VOICES IN THE DIRT

STORIES

IAN CASKEY

RECITAL

Some of the stories in this collection were previously published in different form: "After the Rides" in *BOMB* and *The Strange Recital*, "Man of the Saw" in *Poached Hare*, "The Placenta Tree" in *The Griffin*, and "More Starlight, Please" in *The Strange Recital*.

Cover design by Bryan Maloney
Photo on front cover and title page by Serj Tyaglovsky on Unsplash
Author photo by Bentley Wood

ISBN: 978-1-7337464-6-5
Library of Congress Control Number: 2021946896

RECITAL PUBLISHING
Woodstock, NY 12498
www.recitalpublishing.com

Recital Publishing is an imprint of the podcast The Strange Recital.
Fiction that questions the nature of reality
www.thestrangerecital.com

In loving memory of my friend
Scott Latimore

I never thought of it as God. I didn't know what to call it. I don't believe in devils, but demons I do because everyone at one time or another has some kind of demon, even if you call it by another name, that drives them.

—Gene Wilder

CONTENTS

Can What You Can   1

Jesus Number Two   16

To Planubis with Love   28

Hymn of the Bundy River   47

After the Rides   74

The Placenta Tree   79

Man of the Saw   87

Funerals for Animals   95

More Starlight, Please   117

Hand for Three   128

Still Life of a Used Dessert Fork   138

Jawbone on the Ganges   157

About the Author   191

Acknowledgments   192

More Information   194

CAN WHAT YOU CAN

Henry mashed his cigarette into a tinfoil ashtray. It was full of tar-stinking butts. He crumpled the ashtray closed and, squirming against the passenger door, stuffed the smoldering lump into his jeans like a carcinogenic pocket warmer.

A mid-sixties wind blustered through the front cab windows of the Ford blue truck. I was staring at the Polaroid camera shuddering on the dashboard. Our reflection was faint on the lens, a miniature silhouette, the three of us seated side by side.

We were on our way to Sandy Mush, a green mountain valley with old road beds leading up to hidden, steep slopes, about a thirty-five-minute drive north west of Asheville, North Carolina. Derrick was driving with a fixed grin and one hand slack on the steering wheel. Wire-frame glasses, freshly shaven, he always smelled of Speed Stick by Mennen, original scent. You'd find no butts in his ashtray, the tray fully extended, loaded with coins and Magnails for land surveying. There was still a charred whiff of Henry's butts clinging to the air. Derrick looked past me to glance over at him.

"That bake full of butts ever set your leg on fire?"

"Not yet," Henry said. His brows cramped resolutely behind his black frame glasses. He seemed to be welling up with paternal pride over the lump in his pocket. I joined in.

"You packing that stink-butt egg when you're teaching Comp 101?"

"Packing? No, open carry." A shard of sunlight flared off his glasses. He continued with a nick of slobber building in the corner of his chapped lips. "I show it to them day one, tell them, 'You've got to keep your butts if you're a smoker, just like you've got to keep your vague pronouns and dangling modifiers if you're a writer.'"

There was still an afterimage shard of sunlight swimming inside my eyeballs. Henry grabbed onto a fistful of air. "See, it's all about waste management, proper disposal. You can't just go flicking your butts to the curb. You got to bring them home, flush them down the toilet."

"What about the vague pronouns," I said, "the dangling modifiers?"

"Those you don't flush." He looked to the middle of the road as if in the distance was a troubling presence staring back at him. Then a private thought seemed to crack behind his eyes. He sniffled through the hairy sprigs of his nostrils. His voice became jittery and emotional. "Behind every vague pronoun's an investigation waiting to happen." Then his eyes, bagged with insomnia, sharpened. "It's all about the waste you write and learning how to follow its lead."

I was still thinking of Henry presenting that egg full of cig butts to his students.

"So, you stink up the classroom like that? At an

adjunct level? Man, that's balls. You sure it's not balls you're feeding us?"

"Come to my class and find out."

"That might be awkward," I said.

"Why?" He straightened his glasses.

"I think you know why."

Henry was teaching at the same college where we had all met, and he and Derrick had stayed to graduate and I had dropped out, over eight years ago.

"Who gives a shit about that?" Henry said. "You could audit my class. Sit in back next time I give my spiel on waste management."

"Think I just got front row."

I wiped a speck of Henry's spittle from the side of my cheek. He popped another Winston cigarette in his mouth and struggled against the wind cutting through the window to fire it up. Eventually he prevailed, puffing on his cig with a Unabomber's fervor. We blew past an automotive store with Gosset's Grocery coming up on the right.

"Anybody need anything?" Derrick asked. "Last chance. Only thing I've got on my property is spring water."

I tongued a scrim of lard and a crumble of spicy sausage from the rear of my mouth. We'd all just finished take-out biscuits from Bojangles. All good, we all agreed. Then we shot past Gossett's Grocery and I looked out onto a battered single-wide trailer. There was a large plywood sign propped against a rider mower in the front yard. An advertisement for Y2K canning supplies, the wording neatly stenciled and air-brushed black.

"Prepare. Prepare. Prepare. Can what you can. Y2K. The Day is Nigh."

Nigh as in still a year and a half away. We all agreed that a potential global meltdown over a glitch in two-digit code was a bunch of hooey. Either way, Derrick and Henry were prepared, not with some hideaway cave stocked with jelly jars of pickled okra, green beans, and yeast for probiotic beer, but with a stockpile of their own firearms. Well, Henry only had two firearms, an AMT Hardballer and ASM-DT amphibious rifle, a nineties classic from the Soviet Union. He was ready to barricade himself in his Woodfin home if it came to that. But Derrick—you couldn't even keep up with his arsenal, his most recent purchase being a Heckler and Koch grenade launcher.

He often talked about joining the Army, but you'd think he'd already served. He was a proud member of the N.R.A., and would years later defer his steady progress toward becoming a licensed land surveyor, leaving the small company he worked for as a theodolite operator, to enlist as a paratrooper in the 82nd Airborne Division. Then it would be off to Iraq. Derrick and Henry seemed to have a grip on their future, backing it up with firearms.

My future wasn't as clear as any of that. Working banquets at the Grove Park Inn, ballroom parties, country club weddings, convention buffets. And between shifts, pantry room naps in a dead sector of the hotel, a bottom shelf for a plank-board cot behind a row of gargantuan cans of stewed tomatoes.

There was a time you'd get enough drinks in me and I'd probably bring up my filmmaking aspirations, but the shelf life on that had expired. I'd trashed all my Super

8 films after having them transferred onto a VHS tape, a series of short three-minute reels, but then apartment living on the dark side of a mountain can add a fuzzy green funk of mold to just about anything, my treasured cassette included. Then there was the night after work I invited a ballroom dishwasher to my place to show him my movies, and the VCR just chewed the tape up and spat it back out like squid-ink spaghetti.

It's possible I could've fixed it by winding the tape back into the cassette. But we'd been drinking warthog gin and the warthog said go and get your hammer. Stan the dishwasher shielded himself as I destroyed both the VCR and the cassette. I smashed them up good, cassette chips flying, ribbons of magnetic tape on the hammer jostling like a pom pom. Stan hugged me after that with a manly clap across my back, and then looked at me with amazement in his eyes, as if he'd just witnessed something far superior to anything I could ever have screened on my television. Truth is, you can only watch your own productions so many times before they start failing you. The destruction was justified.

I remember him driving off that night in a souped-up Corolla. A shiny little beast, cherry red, with performance flywheels, high-revving camshafts, and a tailpipe that needed fixing, hanging as it scraped along the asphalt, often sparking like a match scratching to be lit. If I still had my Super 8 camera, I'd have probably asked him to let me use that car in one of my movies. That Corolla had character. Stan, not so much.

Another bump in the road and I was catching Derrick's Polaroid camera as it hopped off the dashboard onto my lap. An instant camera—he said he'd loaded it that morning with a fresh pack of film. I guess you could say I was striving for a comeback of sorts with Derrick's help. What we were setting out to shoot that day wouldn't be a motion picture, but a series of photographs I could lay out on a coffee table like tarot cards, or a scattershot storyboard to a single scene. I asked Derrick what I owed him for the film. He winked at me, said it was on the house.

"Just give me a production credit."

"How about producer?"

"That'll work."

He rocked a fist. Then I could hear the shovels jittering from the truck bed. I started gnawing on a fingernail.

"You look nervous," Henry said after scrubbing a flick of ash into the thigh of his grubby jeans. "You ready to die?"

I smiled back at him.

"Yessir."

But I'm not so sure my smile was all that convincing. My former film projects, the ones I'd revised with the hammer, often involved depictions of myself killing myself. Gunshot spatter on the wall. A sway of legs kicking midair. A plastic bag on my head with the hyperventilating suck coming to a concave end. I preferred black-and-white film where the blood was easy to make with Hershey's chocolate syrup. But this would be in Supercolor 635. Not that the film quality was what had me nervous, but that Derrick and Henry were going to be burying me alive.

It's hard to say if my art was evolving or devolving from death simulations to death approximations. This wasn't going to be a scene in which a corpse would be buried by his killers. I'd been thinking of this more as a Jacques Cousteau of the dirt. Those pantry room naps behind the cans of stewed tomatoes at GPI. That's where the vision had first appeared. Newton had his apple. Bhudda his Bhodi tree. Now I would have my dirt.

Before Derrick and Henry came to pick me up that morning, I'd taken apart my Red Devil vacuum cleaner for parts I'd use as my communication and breathing apparatus, the red flexible tubing for hearing and the adjustable steel pipe for breathing. The noose, the pistol, the insecticide cocktail that had me rabidly foaming at the mouth—those had been campy and fun, macabre films to make. But this...

There was a quaint country house and out in the yard a portable table stacked with fresh ramps for sale, the honor system, two dollars a bunch. Maybe we'd stop by on our way back. You could smell them too, the atomic bomb of the onion/garlic world. Eat a ramp raw and your pits will stink for a week. Derrick was talking up a patch of ginseng he'd found in the upper climes of his land, where we were headed, the mountains deep in the valley, where all roads end.

I returned to my hangnail, gnawing as I sang under my breath with a melodic twang, the opening lines to Slayer's "South of Heaven."

The steep incline of switchbacks along the gravel road leading to the heart of Derrick's property abruptly ended on a long and narrow lot. We were in the middle of twenty-eight acres of forested land, the mountain continuing to rise to the right. Shutting the truck doors, we stretched our legs, backs, and arms. The engine ticked as it cooled down. A lush smell of green trees and vegetation permeated the air, akin to skunk. Most of the trees were tall and healthy, chestnut and scarlet oak, hickory and poplar, a few short and stumpy, paw-paw and sassafras. But it was the taste of mountain air, rich as a moist cake of loam, and the fiddlehead ferns waiting to be snipped, buttered, and pan-sautéed on the red-hot nautilus of an electric stove, that had me wanting to burrow into the earth like a man-sized worm.

Astride the weed-whacked lot was a firewood log pile, topped with an expanse of three blue tarps, the sides of the stacked and quartered logs left exposed for the green wood to season. All of it had been chainsawed and assembled from what had been cleared to make the road. Derrick pointed to where soon he would start building a single-room cabin. Then he pointed back down the road, mentioning a sun-bright area we had passed, where he planned to put a house.

They grabbed the shovels from the truck bed. I followed with the parts I'd removed from my Red Devil vacuum cleaner. Derrick already had a plot in mind, leading us up a path only his eyes could track. Only ten steps climbing dirt, root, and stone, and I was already out of breath. I stopped to spark up a smoke, opening the pearl-snap breast pocket of my blue western shirt. Pack in hand, I tamped out a Lucky Strike. This would be my last cigarette before my friends buried me.

The first puff was dramatic, but not enough for Derrick to take a picture. We continued our upward hike for at least a tenth of a mile. Then with a sweep of the boot, Derrick started clearing a spot on the ground. Henry helped him as I sucked on the last of my smoke. Then I scraped the non-filter out against the craggy face of a nearby boulder, feeling compelled by Henry's presence to store the butt in the cellophane sleeve of my dwindling pack of Luckies.

Now more present than the smell of the surrounding damp forest was the stink of black ash. It was still on my fingertips from having stubbed out my last smoke. Henry jabbed the shovel into the dirt. This was the first picture Derrick took. He placed it on an oak stump to slowly develop. I could see the image starting to appear in a milky dissolve of chemical ephemera. Then I hobbled as I pulled off my sneakers and socks, pants, underpants, shirt, and undershirt. This was going to be a naked affair, except for the Saran Wrap I was going to duct-tape over my face and groin. I wanted all holes covered, except for my mouth and one ear. Then I stepped up to the grave that with each shovel-load continued to deepen before me. The wind blew over my naked skin. It was chillier than expected. I jumped in place, warmed my hands.

Then I started covering my groin, biting off strips of duct tape to adhere the clear wrap to my upper thighs and waist. They continued digging with an automated pace, switching out now and then to work the pit one at a time. I wrapped my face tight enough to smash my nose. I tore holes in the plastic over my mouth and right ear. I taped the wrap where it ended on my neck. The job was done and soon they were done too, standing there, hands relaxed on the grips of their shovels. My friends looked blurry and somber through the shrink wrap, like an antique portrait of gravediggers.

I stepped up to the edge of the pit, sensing its depth: three to four feet deep. There was more than enough room for me to lie comfortably on my back. Henry stabbed his shovel into the earth. It stood alone as he stepped up to me like a bunny rancher with a hand-bolt gun. Playfully, he nudged the twin barrel of his fingers against my temple.

"You ready for this?"

I nodded yes and he offered me a hand, which I accepted by the wrist. Something I'd learned from Derrick, telling me once how movies are full of shit. That a hand won't save anyone from falling from a rooftop or a cliff. You've got to grab them by the wrist. I think that's what had him squinting with a smile from behind the viewfinder. Another flash, another photograph discharged from the mouth of the camera.

The dirt was surprisingly cold. I held the steel pipe upright with the base of it duct-taped over my mouth. Henry pinned the tube leading down to my ear to the outside of the pit with a birch log. I gave them the thumbs up. Derrick took another picture. Henry started shoveling.

Then they both shoveled. Dirt thumped onto my chest. I shut my eyes. They picked up the pace, goading each other on, to see how fast they could accomplish the job. All sense of daylight quickly vanished, and the pressurized build of dirt amassed over time until it felt as though Henry and Derrick had decided to sit on my lungs. That's when the shoveling stopped. I could hear them thwacking the ground flat above me. I imagined the shapes of the spades being imprinted on the dirt, an abstract collection of geometric lines. Henry must've crouched to the ground. His voice sluiced the length of the accordion tubing, filling my ear as if booming into an empty chapel.

"HOW YOU DOING DOWN THERE?"

I could hear Derrick chuckling behind him.

"Fine, except for the ringing in my ear."

I didn't want to tell them how heavy the dirt was against my chest, that'd probably rile them to test the ground above, see if by boot pressure alone they could crack a rib.

"Well, give us a shout if you need anything," Derrick said. "We'll be back after a while."

"Wait, what?"

"I've got some things down at the wood pile to check."

This wasn't something I'd anticipated. I'd always figured they'd wait until I was ready to say I'm done. Maybe they were joking.

"How long will you be gone?"

There was only the soft white noise of the wind whistling down the tube.

"Guys?"

Nothing.

My next breath tasted like burnished steel. It was easy to imagine the carpet dust and grime that had sucked up the length of this pipe at a high velocity. I tried flexing my right hand. I couldn't even move my fingers. *Okay, okay... you've got this.*

The air in the tube was starting to turn stale, yet it was cold enough to evaporate the moisture from the back of my throat, my uvula already starting to feel raw, a soreness that sharpened with every breath.

How stupid I'd been to think the dirt would be toasty as a sleeping bag, when now the earth was working fast to distribute the core of my body heat elsewhere. The bottom of my foot itched. A muscular spasm was threatening to turn into a cramp in the small of my back. Was it possible that I was beginning to breathe more carbon dioxide than oxygen? I was waiting for the tingling sensation of passing out to arrive. But the stark hold of the dirt continued to keep me ice cold and alert.

Then a fleck suddenly appeared on the back wall of my throat. I coughed, unable to swallow. The next several heart beats jumped into my head. I had no idea how far the pipe extended. Could it be that they buried it flush with the ground, so that a strong wind could with great ease sideswipe a handful of dirt down into the pipe. I coughed again, enough for the fleck to hop like a flea. Then I could taste it on my tongue. It wasn't dirt, but a caraway seed from the sausage biscuit that morning. I could see the biscuit in my mind's eye like a buttermilk muppet laughing at me hysterically, *You're gonna die.* The earth was in on it too, starting to suck the heat from my bones. Then came the out-of-body experience, warped as a wide-angle lens. I could see the ground I was buried in, a curvature of dirt surrounding the pipe driving straight down into a crooked show of teeth.

I was there. I was nowhere. I was awake. I was asleep. I was there for a minute. I was there for an hour. It was dark. It was bright. I was breathing. Was I breathing? My throat was burning raw. I was ready. Was I ready? Ready for what?

That's when Derrick said smile and I could sense the electric blue light from the flash bulb piping down into my mouth, and it would look like a picture from the afterlife, my full set of teeth like some unwieldy thing, barely visible down in the pipe, the photograph mildly opaque with an ectoplasmic hue, that without context simply made for a crappy weird picture, one I would absentmindedly leave with a dollar tip at the Waffle House after wolfing down a country ham dinner along with some of the dirt that spilled from my hair.

Henry would waddle ahead of us after that meal as if on the brink of exploding. We'd all had the same dessert, a slice of Southern Pecan pie, while reviewing the pictures Derrick had taken, pictures I would keep after he laced them up in a bowtie of hazard-orange flagging from his land-surveying kit, except for the one I'd left behind, which I can still see, sitting there beside the salt shaker and napkin dispenser. Derrick offered to turn around so I could go and get it, but I told him to keep on driving.

Henry was telling us what he admired about Elizabeth Bishop's poem "The Moose" while I studied the dirt beneath my fingernails. The poem was about a night-time encounter between a busload of passengers and a moose out in the middle of a country road. But it was no ordinary bus, like it was no ordinary moose, not the way Henry described it. What he was talking about was the numinous, where one feels in touch, or within the presence of something divine. Maybe that's what I'd been looking for when I asked them to bury me. But what had I seen? Not much more than what they'd seen in those pictures. And I won't say panicking in the dirt was numinous.

Then there was the traffic coming and going on the Smokey Park Highway. The discussion had moved on to the CIA, MK Ultra tactics, LSD and mind-scrubbing. I was still sitting there, the middle man, listening to the wind as it blustered through the windows.

Their argument centered around mass control. What about self-control? Preservation. I thought about the hammer and all that I'd destroyed. Those films had been dead ends, and properly disposed of at that. Then there was the picture I'd left behind—how if I'd kept it I'd probably never think of it again. I guess that's what constitutes a haunting, something gone still lingering in your mind, or something suddenly there, damp as a cold breath against your neck, or spectral as a luminous figure suddenly vanishing as soon as he appears in the distance. And who was he? Did you see him too? Struggling with a Super 8 camera.

So what if he's gone? Now there were those crooked teeth at the end of the pipe. Sometimes I wake up thinking of them in the middle of the night. The sheets tangled across my legs and arms, my pillow clammy with sweat. It's like those teeth were trying to tell me something. A dark, nervous energy down in the pipe, a voice not quite my own, voices in fact, solemn, yet alive, eager, yet deadpan as someone stating ingredients from a soup can.

Most times, I'll just stare into the dark, and wait to fall back to sleep. But if the voices are loud enough, I'll get up. Sometimes, I'll get dressed, grab a notebook, and drive to the nearest Waffle House on Tunnel Road.

In those after-midnight hours, there's always a booth available like the one I sat at with Derrick and Henry. It's never dark in the Waffle House, a bright yellow interior. The jukebox is rarely ever on. There's just the music of the chef clanging his spatula, and the hiss of cured meat sweating on the grill.

Then there's the warmth of the bottomless cup of

black coffee and my fine-point pen. I'll flex my right hand and wait for the memory of the photograph to slowly drift back into focus, so that I might hear whatever those teeth at the end of the pipe have to say, knowing I've got all night, or rather what's left of it, to write it all down.

JESUS NUMBER TWO

With oven mitts, I thumbed open my creation. Never mind the smoke still fuming from Mama Nina's toaster. There he was in a hatched pod of aluminum foil, a molten Ken doll made shaggy from the ruddy leather I'd grated from a crusty pair of my father's Florsheim shoes.

Mama Nina appeared in the doorway, wagging her arm against the gray smoke, her bracelets jangling, the gloss of her fingernails gleaming blood red. There was some smoke and the overheated stink of burnt shoe leather, vinyl, and plastic. She rushed to a window and threw it open, telling me I could have burned her apartment down.

I was standing there, still waiting for my father to appear. I was eager for him to see my creation. She was waiting for him too, arms akimbo on the hips of her paisley yellow dress, still huffing at me with scorn under her blue eye shadow and stenciled brows.

Mama Nina was my father's girlfriend and they had been drinking that afternoon at Shenanigans, the corner bar, where my father was known as The Poet. They had left me with a massive floor pillow in front of the Zenith

TV. Speed Racer, Johnny Quest, and another boring rerun of Love Boat.

This was 1979.

I was nine years old, on my second summer visit to see Mama Nina and my father in Syracuse, New York. He was a sturdy, stubble-faced thirty-three-year-old, Mama Nina a buxom and hip-heavy thirty-eight. They had both taken the week off to spend with me.

I called her Mama Nina because everyone called her Mama Nina: that was the name of her restaurant on Avon street, known for its Hot Heroes and Angel Hair Florentine. She'd never been married, or had kids, though my father referred to himself as the mistress and her restaurant as the mighty *Marito*.

A Chesterfield cig hung from the corner of his lip as he shuffled up behind her, in a pressed green shirt, unbuttoned at the neck, the starched collar greasy with sweat. Most of his attention was on the beer coaster in his hand, where he continued to scribble on the backside with a Bic pen, probably a fragment of poetry. He did that, scribbling on napkins and matchbooks and the flip side of receipts and unpaid bills.

"What's the fuss?" he said as he gently bumped into Mama Nina, looking up from the coaster. She huffed again, clipping him with her shoulder as she marched out of the kitchen, touching up her hair as if that too could have gone up in flames, her beehive-do with a lock of hair curled aside each cheek.

My father's head was still bobbling from the knock of her shoulder. Now she was in the living room, opening another window. She said, "I want that toaster clean, those shoes off the counter, that mess by the grater gone, and Carl, fix me a Bloody Mary."

But before any of that happened, my father set the coaster down onto the counter. There was a half-drunk look of confusion crimped in one eye against the smoke furling up from his cigarette. He stared at the shaggy, molten creature. I continued to hold it with outstretched arms, proudly displaying my creation on a twin-bed of oven mitts.

I had stripped the Ken doll of his argyle sweater and business slacks. Now he was mutated beyond recognition, into something primitive. His stark blue eyes were still there, along with a distorted grin of bleached white teeth, but the rest of his face was a shaggy profusion of leather.

My father continued to stand there with a baffled grin pushed up his face over what I was holding before him. He even considered for a moment with a raised hand that it might be something he should try and eat. Then he glanced over at his Florsheim shoes beside the toaster, seeing that they had been grated raw. He looked again at my creation. This time more closely, bending forward to see.

"The hell is that?"

"Jesus Number Two," I said with a radiant smile.

The confusion still held over his face, but I knew he'd get it, my creation an inspiration from a movie we had just seen together. I continued to wait for the realization to smack and when it did his expression down-shifted into ample delight. He puffed on his cigarette, a clod of Chesterfield smoke clouding up his head, from the oily thick sweep of his hair down to his chiseled chin. Then he reached with his calloused hand to muss my hair like, *That's my boy, my morbid little genius.*

It was a doll Mama Nina had gifted me and I would apologize to her later, at my father's request, but by then she would know it wasn't an affront toward her so much as transforming a gift she had given me into a gift for my father.

One he would crucify at work, tamp onto the closet wall with three-penny nails, two through the plastic palms and one through the crisscross of feet, a shaggy doll on the lime-green wall overlooking the cleaning products, mop, and roll bucket. Now Jesus Number Two would bless him on his way out the door to give the halls and toilets at Syracuse University a daily shine.

He was first to grab the limp rag from the faucet as we turned our attention to scrubbing down the kitchen, leaving it spotless with a gleam, spritzing the air with an aerosol hiss of Lysol, long after he fixed Mama Nina her Bloody Mary.

I never mentioned the ashes we had missed, the ones that had drifted from the tip of his Chesterfield smoke, a dirty gray pinch of ashes tucked alongside the running board under the sink cabinet door. But I still see the ashes there, and looking back, sometimes it's all I see.

***

The idea for Jesus Number Two had come from a movie at the ACME duplex on Butternut Road. During my week visit with Mama Nina and my father, we would go to the ACME most nights, switch-hitting between two films, one on the big screen, one on the little, *All That Jazz* and *Wise Blood*. This was back when movies rated PG were really rated R and rated R movies were okay for kids to see. And it was more of a ritual, a cozy getaway, those springy seats you could throw your back into for a good bounce.

There were character quirks to the leading men in both films that matched the resilient mania of my father. My father also liked to smoke in the shower like the dance choreographer Bob Fosse did in *All That Jazz*. My father also believed the Bible was a bunch of hooey like Preacher Motes did in *Wise Blood*.

But it was Enoch Emory who fascinated me most after he stole the shrunken body of a petrified man from a museum to present to Preacher Motes as the New Jesus. That's what had me the following day cooking up Ken in Mama Nina's toaster.

My father insisted on calling the doll Barnabas instead of Jesus Number Two. He declared Barnabas a much more interesting man, the impenitent thief, the one crucified to the left of Jesus.

"Not the penitent one," he sharply added, "but the one nobody really knew. The nameless one, the one who rebuked Christ, saying, 'If you're such a savior then why can't you save yourself?' Unlike the penitent thief, who was nothing more than a last-minute suck-up to Christ, just some chump looking for salvation at the checkout line. Barnabas was a thief, knew he would always be a thief, on into the afterlife."

"I think you're getting your names mixed up," Mama Nina said after we settled into our bouncy seats to see *Wise Blood* for the third time.

"Wasn't Barnabas a saint?" she said.

"No, no, no," my father said after cracking open a can of Stroh's to slurp at the foam before he handed me the pull-tab so I could wear it like a prize ring. That curled tab of aluminum was like a razor tongue, one that could cut the hand of anyone digging too close to mine in the family bucket of popcorn.

My father fidgeted, an abrasive shriek wincing from the springy seat as he suppressed a belch, the sound of it fizzing inside his ribs as his eyes widened. "He was the bad thief. The nameless thief. The one everyone should remember. It was Barnabas who truly suffered."

Then the theater darkened and my father looked at the movie screen as if beyond it he could see everything that Barnabas had endured.

"Do you even know what you're talking about?" Mama Nina said, emptying her Red Hot Tamales along with my Milk Duds into the family bucket of popcorn. "You say he's nameless, yet his name's Barnabas?! I mean what kind of sense is that? Besides, Barnabas wasn't a thief."

"Aww, what would you know about it?" my father said.

"A lot," she said. "I am Catholic after all, and Barnabas was the son of consolation."

"Consolation? Malarkey."

Mama Nina narrowed her eyes.

She said, "You can't stand being wrong, can you?"

Someone shushed us from behind.

"That's right," my father said, angling an arm toward the screen with his can of Stroh's. "Movie's about to begin, so hush."

Though Mama Nina and my father never married, they certainly acted like it, and I loved sitting between them at the movies, even when their hands bullied around mine in the bin of popcorn for Milk Duds and Red Hot Tamales, and as for the prize ring, well, it never drew blood, but it did bring about a surprised gasp once from Mama Nina that had my father and me tittering in the dark.

***

Shortly after my summer visit in the fall of '79 my father had a manic episode, losing his job at Syracuse University as head custodian, for publicly jousting a baffled and unarmed Raymond Carver with a mop.

My father was convinced that Mama Nina and Raymond Carver, who was teaching at Syracuse at the time, were having an affair, because Raymond was frequently dining at Mama Nina's, persistently fawning over her garlic bread and wild scungilli sauce, and who knows, maybe they *were* having an affair.

According to my father, Raymond was still laughing it off, until my father rammed him a second time with the mop. "Blam, in the solar plexus!" My father used to brag. Then the two men openly brawled in front of the Hall of Languages, resulting in a bloody lip for Raymond and a broken pinky for my father.

That night, thunderously packing the backseat of his avocado Dodge Dart with an armful of clothes and an electric baby blue typewriter atop a case of Stroh's, my father, destined for Los Angeles, forced Mama Nina into an impulsive, last-minute choice, either him or her crummy restaurant.

***

It's been over thirty years since they have spoken. I still cringe thinking of the love letter he mailed me to give to her when I was ten years old. My father had moved to Venice Beach, California after Mama Nina chose her restaurant over him. The following summer he knew my mother and I were going to be driving through Syracuse to visit my grandparents in Niagara Falls. He thought, I figured, if I delivered the letter to Mama Nina, instead of mailing it himself, that it might boost his chances for rekindling his relationship with her.

At first, I found the letter upsetting, because there wasn't anything in the envelope addressed to me, except for a lemon yellow post-it inside the envelope that read, "Hey Rich, Give this to Mama Nina!"

My mother insisted I throw the letter away after we read it together at the kitchen table. It was a love letter she critiqued like one of my school papers.

"It's hardly legible, though the sentiment is clear. It's infested with clichés, and lines swindled from Pablo Neruda," which she knew, because she had read some of those lines to him when they had been married.

"*I love you as the plant that doesn't bloom... darkly in my body as I lie upon your floor with my head at the foot of your kitchen stove—*

"I mean what is that?!" My mother snapped her hand against the letter. "Well, your father always aspired to be a great writer, one stolen line at an inebriated time, sadly adding God knows what tripe of his own."

And from where I was standing by my mother's side, all I saw was an apologetic letter full of love and pain and pledges to be a better man. Instead of throwing it away, she deposited the letter in a Ziplock bag like a queasy piece of criminal evidence, taking it away from me, which made me feel that I had betrayed my father, and sowed in me that hot sticky afternoon a seedling of hatred for my mother.

She never asked what I had wanted to do with the letter, and I would have never shown it to her had she not been the one to take it from the mailbox.

**

I remember the following afternoon, canning a dollop of feces in a jelly jar. This was after puncturing a series of holes in the screw-top lid with an ice pick. Before hiding the jar in a storage box beneath her bed, I added a pinch of coarse salt to embolden the scent.

Looking back now, I realize it was a cruel and odd and rebellious act. I did it, I think, in honor of my father as a perverse form of retaliation. My mother always sniffed it out ever so faintly in her room, a damp and troubling taste.

Several agitated nights in a row, we searched for what it could be. At the dresser, while she was rooting around her bed, I pretended to accidentally drop one of her favorite figurines, a keepsake from her childhood, a porcelain hobo with a clown-faced smile. The sound of its head breaking on the hardwood floor was enough to divert her from continuing her search beneath the bed.

She never found what was stinking up her room, persistently spraying for months with a lavender mist before accepting the soiled odor as part of her bedroom.

I never told my father or anyone about the jelly jar of feces, something my mother discovered years later, a petrified pebble of absolute mystery, a dehydrated nugget, bone hard and salty white, one that she rolled out onto the kitchen table like an ivory die.

"Do you know anything about this?"

"No," I shrugged.

And as for the letter, I told my father I had delivered it to Mama Nina, which my mother did on our way to Niagara Falls. This also included my mother showcasing love letters my father had written to her as well. In Mama Nina's living room, I recall the two of them comparing notes while I was supposedly watching television in Mama Nina's bedroom.

A rerun of *Gilligan's Island*, Gilligan all alone in his white bucket hat, lanky red shirt, white pants, and sneakers, reluctantly wandering into a spooky cave. The ginger ale Mama Nina had given me was flat, and her laughter barreled into the room followed by my mother's mousy giggle.

I was still standing, half-sitting on the end of Mama Nina's four-poster bed, which was neatly made, as was the rest of her room, everything meticulously ordered and dusted with the sheen of a lemony scent as if expecting a photographer from *Homes and Antiques* magazine, and on the wall above the wood-paneled television on the mahogany dresser was a picture of Naples, Italy, gilded in a floral frame, with sail boats and fishing boats on an aqua-blue coastline.

It was a place my father had promised, one cockeyed summer night, we would all go, as he danced like Bob Fosse in front of Mama Nina and me while we lay on her bed, my father singing of the carp we would catch, and the spaghetti *frutti di mare* and *vongole* we would eat, until his wild, swinging dance hipped up against the dresser, knocking the lamp to the floor, throwing the fantasy, with the three of us as a family casting a fishing net off the coast of Naples, in the dark.

It could have been that the Professor, Mr. and Mrs. Howell, the Skipper, and the girls were trapped in that cave, swaddled in a massive web. I don't remember, except that there was a five-hundred-pound spider that had Gilligan running back out of the cave. The spider spat his white bucket hat out into the light of day, too frightened to scuttle further out of the cave. That hairy, gigantic spider reminded me somehow of Jesus Number Two and that jelly jar of feces I had hidden under my mother's bed.

"From the shit we talk, to the shit we give, to the shit we secretly smear on each other," my father once said on the heels of a rant, his inebriated tone not unlike a preacher.

I wanted that afternoon to hide something in Mama Nina's bedroom too, something that would reek to eternity. I *did* set the ginger ale on the dresser, skipping the coaster, hoping the pearls of sweat sliding down the glass would stain the finished wood. Then I looked around the room for something to take. I walked up to a display of necklaces—each one had a crucifix, some silver, others gold, most of them tiny.

Soon we were out on the highway with the sound of

the wheels humming on the road. My mother and I agreed it was nice seeing Mama Nina. I sat with my arm hanging outside the passenger door. I was squeezing what I'd stolen, perhaps hoping for a dramatic streak of blood to appear. Then I leaned my head outside the window. My mother told me to get back into my seat. It didn't matter—what I'd stolen, I could keep it, or throw it away. What mattered was that I had become a thief. I resettled in my seat. The wind continued to howl across the window. My hands were empty. The future seemed vast, nothing but wild open country.

TO PLANUBIS WITH LOVE

The message was full of cellular interference, but it was clear Alejandro had tried to kill himself. He was calling from a psych ward, which one was unclear, lost in a glitch. He was all snot and sniffles, apologizing for ruining our trip. The fucker. The whole reason I had flown to L.A. from North Carolina was so we could go on a camping trip.

I had just landed and was on my way to the car rental agency. The shuttle bus windows rattled all around me. That California sun on the billboards and the palm trees looking now like a fast pass to skin cancer.

"Three days. Big Sur. Redwoods. Pacific coast. Bald eagles, bro! Get your ass out of that slump, yo!" That's how he had pitched the trip three weeks ago. I was getting over a breakup. A seven-week relationship, my longest ever. I loved her. Still do. But since the breakup more than nine months ago she had ghosted me, blocked me, even threatened me with a restraining order.

So memo with anthrax received!

And I mean from her to me, because I would never. See, when you truly love someone—even when they press delete on everything you send them—you will always want the best for them, even when they leave you for a tech-savvy girlfriend. She'd been seeing her when we were going out, and I will give her this, that she'd always been up front about it, never once saying we were exclusive.

They do make a fine pair. They've started a business together too. A micro-brewery. Last I checked, their GoFundMe page had capped its goal. So congrats on that! Soon you'll be seeing their brew on the market. A milky stout. The alternative to Guinness. Joan of Arc, Joan of Stout, something like that. I'd like to think my anonymous contribution was the one that got them over the finish line.

Either way, doing that for them was like healing, you know. It was a sizable contribution too. It took maxing out a fresh credit card to slam dunk that 5k. So, did that contribution help clear the existential gloom of our breakup? No, but it was a start, because like I said, true love is only wanting the best for those you lose, and I mean WANTING, even when they've completely erased you from their life.

Crazy, right?

I know.

So how about pouring me a pint of Joan of Stout, because if anyone should've been checking themselves into a psych ward it should've been me. Those Big Sur trails were supposed to be my savior, the Pacific coast my soul cleanser, the crash and boom of those waves the body slam that would free me of her.

Of course, I could go it alone. Take the 101 solo to Big Sur. Or hit an L.A. beach for at least half the experience. But my trip was already starting to curdle. Like let's fly back tonight. I would have done it too, except there was one other thing. A solid Alejandro had requested. He wanted me to take care of his goldfish, Parsons.

***

The plan had been to rent a compact car for the drive to Big Sur since Alejandro's Subaru was an overheating shit-box. But when I reached the counter I was no longer in a compact-car frame of mind. This was my first time in The City of Angels. I was going to hit it in style. I drummed my hands on the counter, told the rep, "I want a muscle car. Something fast and furious." I was waiting for the right-away-sir smile instead of a sober-faced damage-waiver advisory.

"Nope." I said. "Just the keys."

And it was all hot rod, banana yellow with a sleek muscular finish, chrome rims and a growler of a tailpipe. The bucket seats were low, as in feel-your-ass-humming-over-the-asphalt low. Now I won't say revving the engine took the combustion out of Alejandro bailing on our trip, but it did feel good flooring it into drive, only to find L.A.'s reputation for bumper-to-bumper traffic gruelingly true.

Interstate 10 was jammed, coming and going. What should have been a breezy twenty minutes to East Hollywood turned into a numb-butt throbbing from my sitz bone. Tap and go, tap and go, an endless Western Avenue. Then it was another red light, watching the traffic cross in front of me, Glenn Frey cooking up a classic on the radio, "You Belong to the City".

There was someone shouting over to my right. A homeless guy with a dirty tanned face and frizzy hair. He was arguing with a curbside waste can. Then a man with dung-matted tendrils of hair popped out of the garbage. He had on a yacht captain's hat. He was staring down at the treasure in his hands: a half-eaten box of fried chicken. The fight was on. The two men like Spartacus for the feed. Bones jumped from their hands and the box ripped. Then they were on their hands and knees, snuffling for the meatiest piece. The Captain sprang upright, a plump thigh in his hand.

His back-strut shuffle before taking the first savage bite reminded me of Alejandro, who was also scrawny and muscular with crude facial features and wolf-hair eyebrows verging on a unibrow. Had these two street warriors also moved out here to pursue a dream? No doubt, the fever was in their eyes, like nuggets of California gold they would one day possess with the same fervor they applied to gnashing meat from the bone.

**

Alejandro's dream was to write, direct, produce, and star in his own movies, and when we were roomies in Asheville we had penned a screenplay together. We finished it in under seventy-two hours, no sleep, grinning like champs. We wrote it on six pitchers of iced coffee a day, and half a bottle of Adrenaloxin—an organic speed that gave us laser focus, bugged-out eyes, and stopped-up bladders, so we were puking coffee from our nostrils, once on the keyboard, which miraculously didn't short circuit, except for a finicky J button that kept repeating itself. Sun up, sun down, we kept clacking on the keys, those repeater Js be damned. Then the concussive blow from scribing a masterpiece put me to sleep for close to seventeen hours.

Alejandro had the whole thing printed and stapled: our doomsday, sci-fi epic, over three hundred pages, easily half the length of a trilogy—*The Seed Hunters*. He proudly entered the title and our names into the Internet Movie Data Base. We marveled over that for at least a day, the synopsis of our masterwork there online for everyone to see.

The Seed Hunters. Set on the matriarchal planet of Planubis ("pronounced Pla-NOO-bis" we wrote on IMDB), where all the women have been genetically modified to produce more women, and women only, and all the men have been eradicated, their seed stored in a metallic ovoid building, known as The Bank. When a group of terrorists in floppy penis masks bomb The Bank, Planubis is thrown into a quandary. What will they do for seed?

Fast forward thirty-three years (and if you're thinking why thirty-three, not thirty, or twenty-nine, that's good! And even better if you're thinking thirty-three: that's how old Christ was when he died and was resurrected; now you're really tuning into the subtext of the film, so if you've got that, major points, because that's what we're looking for, an audience that KNOWS how to pick up on the coded subtleties within a film, and believe me, *The Seed Hunters* is packed full of them, rabbit holes galore) and the looming threat of extinction is still ticking as loud as a time bomb when a weary yet manly signal arrives from a distant planet known as Testilicos. That's when the film really begins, with a group of seven women loading up into a tinfoil spaceship... on the hunt... for seed.

Sure, we knew it was ambitious material, possibly offensive, super campy. The plan was to make it on a Sharknado budget. There were still some industrial sites around Asheville. Alejandro had a girlfriend at the time, too, ready to play the lead role, Aura Nothis. Of course, we never thought it would propel us to stardom, though secretly we did, and then not so secretly, always after two or three beers, already quoting from our own film as if we'd already made it and the world had seen it several times over.

Either Alejandro or I, or the two of us in unison would quote Aura Nothis (pronounced Not His, though often mispronounced throughout the film as an annoyance to Aura as: Know This). She's the trusty space captain from Planubis (with—*spoiler alert here*—a "they/them" secret of her own) so we would always quote her with our arms akimbo and chins jutted to the side, even sometimes dressing up like her in silver latex and blonde wigs. We'd give it our best Nothis accent.

"Testilicos is our only hope."

"True that."

Clunk, we'd toast a couple of Pabst cans.

Then Alejandro moved to L.A.

The Seed Hunters never came up again. I think he wanted to branch off and do his own work. He was the one who'd always been more serious about filmmaking than me. I just figured, why not give it a shot. But for him it was everything and that never wavered, judging from the heart in his eyes. But hey, we were still in our late thirties, so you never know, until you do know, but on that flight out to L.A. I didn't know, and what I could see of the city beyond the wing of the plane and that huge turbine was enough to make me think there was a place down there where my name might shine.

That was after the turbulence, the kind requiring you to keep your seatbelt fastened, and I'm not a religious person but I should've kept my head tucked between my knees, praying to the good lord. There was a kid across the aisle who had been filming me with his phone. His mother apologized but I told them it was okay.

I even asked to see the video. The picture was jittery, my face flushed red as I proceeded to slam forward again and again as the turbulence struck. There were several other passengers looking back at me like I was having a seizure, and I was having a seizure of sorts, maybe even exploiting the moment to express some subconscious turbulence of my own. I handed the phone back to the kid and told him to give me a cut of the likes if the video ever went viral. Really, I didn't mind his filming me. I even thought it was funny, feeling somewhat proud of having the humility to crack a smile over seeing a video of myself in the throes of a dying pandemonium. Then there was the view of L.A. soon followed by the plane landing and the voice mail from Alejandro.

You don't ever realize how much you're banking on something until the bank goes bust. I thought I was thinking about the camping trip, but maybe what I had really been thinking about was to reignite this partnership, find backers for *The Seed Hunters*, and get it up on the silver screen. Or at least streaming online.

I think I was also harboring the dream of my ex hearing about it. How I had moved to L.A. and *boom* was suddenly a viral sensation. Alejandro had said he was working on something big, though I knew he was still working full-time as an oil tech at Jiffy Lube (the great irony of letting his Subaru turn into an overheating shit box, which I suspect also had subconscious roots of its own—in his case coming from his troubled relationship with his Japanese father).

But back to the dream—as in one day you're changing someone's oil and the next they're watching your latest hit on Click Fix. If anything, I thought it would just be fun to talk up the idea while we were out on the trail. I'd give Alejandro the Planubian hand salute. We'd see where it would go from there. Three nights of Big Sur would have been plenty of time to dream up the second half of our trilogy. But apparently there'd been something else on his mind. Razors and a hot bath.

I had just talked to him two days ago. He said he was pumped, PUMPED to hit the trail. Maybe he was already pumped on synthetic weed, diablo head rush, or dusted kratom. He'd been dropping hints about bringing some such shit on the trail, something that'd skull-boost our brains higher than the redwoods. Could have been he just couldn't hold back on the party before I got there, smoking himself up into some paranoid delusional state.

Getting high for us was always a spin of the roulette wheel. A seventy-percent chance your ball was going to land on a cold sweat of exponential self-loathing, but you do it anyway, because there's a thirty-percent chance you'll smoke yourself off the wheel into a giddy cosmological shrug toward existence. But that seventy-percent shock zone was where it often landed unless we were together to talk ourselves out of the hallway of shattered mirrors.

I suppose I could try and find him. Maybe there was a way to ping his voice mail. So much of what he'd said had been lost to the interference. I could google psych wards. But I bet there are forty psych wards for every talent agency in L.A. So good luck with that. Also, if he wanted me to find him, he'd call again. I knew he had family too—a sister in Ohio, parents he loathed in Vermont. His father had been the conductor of the Japan Philharmonic Orchestra, and had moved on to teaching—an intense man with bushy white hair who seemed persistently perturbed by an unacceptable smell. I'd only met him once.

At a Latin Fusion restaurant in Lebanon, New Hampshire, Alejandro told me before dinner that we would all have to wait until his father picked up his silverware to begin eating. But we were so stoned, I totally spaced out and picked up my silverware first, and then his father left the table along with the rest of Alejandro's family.

The restaurant was packed so they had to wait for another table to clear before having their food reheated and served again. Me, I carried my plate and kept on eating. After dinner in the parking lot, Alejandro applauded me for being so bold. I told him it was the chronic we'd smoked, dusted with F.U.B.A.R., that had commanded my appetite. "So, don't thank me, thank the weed."

***

It was 4:30 west-coast time, the east-coast dinner bell clanging in my gut. A speed bump chafed under the car as I pulled up to the menu board at Carl's Jr. Had I not been going fast enough my ride would have been stuck on the speed bump. I could already see the counter person at the car rental agency telling me again with delight in her eyes, *You should have got the damage waiver.* But a low rider's a low rider and I'll fight that in court. Not that I've got a credit card to max out for a lawyer. I think I maxed my credit to the limit donating that 5k to Joan of Stout. This trip was gratis ala Visa as well. I was looking at two, maybe three years in a penguin tux working banquets at the Grove Park Inn to pay it all off. I could always represent myself if it came to that, don my dinner coat and tie, flatten my hand on the Bible, swear to tell the truth.

"It's the car's fault, your honor."

But I was overthinking it, the drive-through voice on the intercom asked again for my order. There it was: the Beyond Famous Burger. Man, everyone here is so starved for fame they even named a burger that goes beyond it all. Like here it is, everything you wanted and more. Kudos to Carl's Jr. for profiting on that. I couldn't wait to see what's so beyond about it. I ordered mine with cheese. Then there was the open road, and my hand reaching into the bag. The fucking fries were cold, as in dead cold, the burger too. I guess that's what they mean when they say beyond, as in beyond the grave. Uneatable crap. I'd get something else later.

But the Coke float was righteous, a thick draw through the straw. I sucked hard. There was Phil Collins on the radio, brooding on a synth pad, his voice calling out against the occasional cry of a Fender guitar, the spit of the drum machine mounting in subtle calculation. Here was a man about to whomp on the toms, speaking from where "the pain still grows."

I mean, come on! Put a Coke float on that and see where it takes you. There was Phil telling me to "Hold on," or was he saying, "Oh Lord"? Then the traffic signal ahead turned yellow and I took it to mean hold on and I did... goosing the gas.

**

Have you ever been to a crime scene? Sure, you've seen dozens of them on TV and in the movies. I'm not saying anyone was murdered, but that's what it looked like when I stepped into Alejandro's bathroom.

There was blood everywhere. The cheap plastic shower curtain pulled from the rod, a crumpled mass on the floor. The bath water was stagnant, a ruddy gray. I imagined Alejandro lying there, idling his time as he bled out into the tub. The bathroom started to spin all around me and I slammed out into the living room.

Outside, I rushed down the concrete stairs to dry retch over the sidewalk. I was still dizzy. I settled on the front lawn. I stared at one of the palm trees. Then I held my face in my hands. I thought I could hear a swarm of mosquitoes coming toward me. Then I saw it hovering above me, almost within reach—a quadcopter drone with a camera eye.

I struggled to stand, while it maintained an invasive yet unreachable distance. I looked up and down the street, at every neighboring window, seeing no one. Then I swatted at the drone and gave it the finger. Its camera was still trained on me, as it zipped up into the sky to veer out of sight.

It was much faster than I could follow. I steadied myself at the base of the outer stairs. My hand on the railing, I looked up to Alejandro's front door. Maybe this was all part of some prank. The next big thing Alejandro had been talking about. Some whacked-out YouTube shit. Part of the reaction-shot craze. Like that kid on the airplane filming me with his phone. I wouldn't put it past Alejandro to do the same. *Check it! Here's a video of my friend freaking after he sees the bathroom where he thinks I've attempted suicide.* I wanted to see a small film crew arrive with Alejandro leading them with open arms to give me a hug. *You've been pranked.* But it never happened.

There was still blood on the walls. I closed the bathroom door and pulled out my phone. Surely, I could drum up something on Airbnb or Couchsurfer. Find another place to stay. I sat at the only chair at the dinette table. There was Parsons in his fishbowl at the other end of the table.

What a weird looking fish. How he could keep that knobby head and puffball of a body circulating with those dinky fins seemed a miracle. I tapped the glass. He seemed unperturbed by my presence. Had he been a dog he would have either been whimpering for food, or yapping because I was a stranger. But he was a goldfish, exotically deformed, and indifferent to the world outside the bowl. Maybe that was part of the appeal of having him as a pet. Those globular eyes never blinking, always placid, whether you're boiling up some ramen on the stove, or whipping it to some porn on the sofa, or getting wheeled out on a gurney.

"It's all the same to you, right, little buddy?"

He continued to swim round and round. I looked out into the living room, a Goodwill sofa, a backpack half-full and propped against the wall next to a pair of musty hiking boots. That's when I stood from the table and started to scream.

I was screaming at Parsons. I was screaming at Alejandro. I was screaming at my ex. Then I just stood there, breathing. The proof was in the fishbowl. Parsons unfazed. The ultimate little buddha, no thought or feeling. That he seemed unaffected by my screaming made me feel okay. Perhaps he was there to absorb my toxicity. Those bulbous eyes looking at me as if to say, *There is nothing but swim.*

Thank you, Parsons. Thank you. I gave him a curt bow then fed him from the container next to the bowl. He swam up to the surface, nibbling at the fish flakes with a gruesome underbite. That was Parsons taken care of, for now.

There was a flat screen TV on the wall, a scatter of DVDs on an entertainment console, *Life is Beautiful, Horrible Bosses, Shame,* and Bertolucci's *The Dreamers.* Maybe I would stay at Alejandro's, order up some

Chinese, watch a flick or two, pass out on the sofa. Then there was the most terrific squeal.

I rushed to the window. There was still a trace of black-tire smoke over the street. I surveyed the cars parked along the curb, and then the blow came, striking me dead-center in the chest. My hot rod was gone. I gripped the sill, and leaned even further out the window. There was nothing to see, except for the tire streaks on the road. Then I just stared at where I had parked the car until another one filled the space. Now I could imagine the counter woman at the car rental agency telling me flat-out I was fucked.

I spanked the DVDs off the entertainment console. What was I going to do?! Was I going to call the police? Have them draft up an incident report, which would just be a proof of purchase for a stolen car. I kicked at the crappy sofa. I wouldn't even be here if it wasn't for Alejandro. Then there was Parsons swimming round and round in his fishbowl. You want me to take care of your fish?! Oh, I'll take care of your fish.

I swept up the bowl, lifting it over my head. Water splashed down the back of my hair. Time to say hello to the wall! Then my rage skipped a beat. Something had caught my eye from Alejandro's bedroom. A silver glint on the floor. I returned Parsons to the dinette table. The door to Alejandro's room was half open.

Slowly, I entered. There was a poster of the famous Hollywood sign torn from the wall and trampled on the floor. Next to it was the silver husk of a unitard. I picked it up, bringing it to my face. It smelled of Alejandro, a sandalwood musk over a stale oniony sweat. An early evening shaft of light spilled through the dirty window. I sat on a kicked-over milk crate. The unitard, still in my hands, was silver as a space-orbit suit. I stared at the motes swirling through the shaft of light. Aura Nothis.

***

When an attractive person smiles at you from a distance, there is hope, but when a youthful group collectively becomes giddy after smiling at you, there is the feeling that you've somehow marked their day with a humorous and whimsical aside, perhaps worthy of a post, or something they'll share with someone else later in the day.

It's true, I was still wearing yesterday's clothes, now stained at the pits. I'm sure I had a bit of sofa bed head too. Parsons was all the charm I had, the fishbowl cradled in my arms. He was motoring around, proudly swishing his coat-tail fin. There was the ocean-front walkway, Venice Beach. The group seated outside the Wee Chippy joint at a picnic table were now privately conferring among themselves while plucking from a communal box of chippy fries.

I would have to tell Alejandro about the smiles Parsons had attracted before I set him free. I'd already placed an order at the take-out window, eager to nosh on my own box of Loch Ness Chips with malt vinegar and nutritional yeast.

I glanced back at the foursome at the table with a sun-in-your-eyes squint. The girl with a red stripe in her hair was showing off a tattoo she had on the inside of her lower lip. I wasn't close enough to read it, watching the hand of another girl as she dipped a fry into a specialty sauce. I could smell it, too, faint on the wind, a tangy chipotle BBQ sauce. My stomach grumbled.

"You got another card?" The window clerk said. "This one's been declined."

"Try again," I said, and again it was declined. Several swipes later the Wee Chippy clerk said, "Sorry, bro. Got any cash?"

But I'd spent my last fifteen dollars on take-out from Wah's Golden Hen. My card had worked with Lyft, or had it? I needed to look at my phone. I stepped away from the counter and placed Parsons on the ground. My phone wouldn't power up. I guess I'd forgotten to charge it. I was still a little foggy after having painkillers for dessert last night, baby blue pills I'd discovered in Alejandro's medicine cabinet. My tongue was dry as sandpaper.

I could hear the waves in the distance, the white wash of the ocean crashing on the shore. I kept my gaze on the palm trees and the blue open sky as I wandered closer to the picnic table, looking as if in thought. The group seemed sketched out, now that I didn't have Parsons in the crook of my arms. Maybe they thought I was waiting for a hit of their fries like a nearby seagull. One of the girls suggested they leave and they started to stand up from the table. Hopefully, not on my account. Then they were gone and I gave the blue sky a set of prayer hands. They'd thrown a third of their french fries away. A third! The box was on top of a waste can for the picking.

I swooped up to the feast, jarred by the sudden appearance of a scraggly male Medusa. That crazed look in his eyes turned me to stone. The box was his, and oh, was he a fast eater, already with a mouthful of fries sprouting from his lips. I sharpened my eyes, preparing for battle. My fist tightened. He was still jamming fries into his mouth. A seagull landed nearby, cawing with laughter.

This man, he looked familiar. Was this the East Hollywood dude I'd seen yesterday scrapping for chicken bones? He had the same dung-matted hair, though the captain's cap was missing. I was pretty sure it was him. The one who had reminded me of Alejandro. My fist loosened. I continued to stare at him.

There was a three-man band marching along the ocean-front walkway, trombone, sax, and a big-booming drum. That's when I rushed up to the Captain to give him a brotherly hug. His mouth was still stuffed with fries. He shoved me away, clutching the box tightly with a pugilist's grunt. I told him he reminded me of a friend. He told me to fuck off, said if I touched him again he'd end me. Then the trombone blew a bum note, but the band kept marching on.

***

The time had come to take care of Parsons. We were waist deep in the ocean. The size of the waves was increasing with intensity. I was surprised to still have the fishbowl in the crook of my arm. The little dude had caught another set of smiles too. His newest fans a couple of surfers. One with a GoPro camera strapped to her wrist, the other with a GoPro strapped to her helmet. They were both just up ahead, yelling back at me. The ocean was almost too loud to hear them.

"What's that?" I said.

The gap-toothed surfer said, "What are you doing with that fish?" The other surfer with fusilli hair said, "That fishbowl's a hazard. You need to get out of the water."

"No, no, it's fine," I shouted. "I'm going to set him free."

"But that's a freshwater fish, you idiot! He'll die."

I hadn't thought of that. Then a wave smacked over the entire scene. A tremendous force sucked me under. Have you ever had your face violently scraped across the ocean floor? When the undercurrent finally released me, I felt I had fallen from the sky onto the beach. I was coughing up salt water. The surfers were further out into the ocean. Then the fishbowl pushed up onto the shore. I scampered up to it, picking it up. There was water and sand in the bowl. Parsons was gone.

I surveyed the ocean all the way to the horizon line. A burn of salt water trickled from my nose. My hope was that he had lived long enough to see the ocean as a wondrous place brimming with possibility. Then another wave fizzled before my toes. I dumped the water from the fishbowl, leaving the inside streaked with sand. Then I studied the bowl, realizing how much it looked like an astronaut's helmet.

The opening was large enough to cram my head inside it. The sound of my breathing now surrounded me. Those two surfers were out there making their movie. A total success! It was glorious to see, the two of them slicing down the face of the same wave. I gave them the Planubian salute.

Then I looked out onto the waves forming behind them, one beginning to build into a rising crest before it came crashing down. Maybe now I could start my vacation. Securing the glass globe round my head with both hands, I sprinted out into the shallows, rushing for the deep. There is nothing but swim.

HYMN OF THE BUNDY RIVER

Remember Dudley T. Edger? That oil man, gas man, farty CEO of his own billion-dollar company. What about that crude-oil lake he used to own in Oklahoma? The one with the casino resort. What was it called? *Bella Mi Fanghi*, which, I think, translates from the Italian to something like beauteous mud. Remember how he called it the eighth wonder of the world? And what about that wacky commercial? The casino bling. The kiddie rides. The infinite buffet. That chorus line of women dressed up like baked potatoes and busty prime ribs, dancing beneath a holy choir suspended midair, jangling tambourines. Then there was Mr. Edger in his cash-green suit telling you to make this your summer destination. My father loved that commercial. He'd fidget in his cozy chair while it played on the television, a hand tucked under the belt-line of his pants. Then he'd crane his neck to tell my mother and me we should really make a point of going there someday. But this isn't a story about a family vacation to *Bella Mi Fanghi*. This is a story about how Mr. Edger poured into our lives like an oil slick. But before we get to that you should know a few things about my father and our family history.

This was 1983. I was eleven years old. We lived in Sewell, Oklahoma, a rural and weedy no-man's land, closer to Enid than Stillwater. I was an only child, therefore spending a lot of time alone, skipping flat stones across a nearby creek, or cupping my hands together to whistle between my thumbs like a mourning dove. Above the flower-print sofa in our living room was an oil-painting of a Krakow castle. I'd often stand and stare at that stony castle, wondering what it'd be like to wander those halls. We didn't have Krakow royalty in our blood, but my father was Polish, and had grown up in Krakow, and had learned dentistry from his father, who'd been a labor-camp dentist in World War II, specializing in extractions, something he'd been forced to do as a means of survival, extracting gold teeth for the Germans.

My father had moved to America when he was a young man to make a name for himself, and that name was Dr. Martin Młot. A name that his dental patients often mispronounced. He told me how they pronounced the "ł" in our last name like the English "l" in lot, luck, and love, instead of how it phonetically sounds like the English "w" in warm, water, and waste. But he never corrected them, wanting them to feel at ease before he drilled into their mouths. His private practice was on the outskirts of Enid, and of the two billboards and the one fifteen-second commercial spot that ran for Młot's Dentistry between game show reruns of *The Joker's Wild* and *Press Your Luck* his business continued to slump in profits.

Then there was his incessant grumbling over the

agony of performing third-molar extractions and the early onset of what some in the industry call "lock claw," where sudden bouts of rheumatoid arthritis would cause his hand to seize up into a claw. He was only thirty-seven years old. His right hand should've had at least another decade of hard use, performing extractions, filling cavities, installing crowns. But the arthritic attacks were becoming more frequent.

He refused to see an orthopedic doctor, hiding his hand whenever it cramped up, tucking it behind his back, or in his pants pocket. And if it happened at dinner, he would eat one-handed with downcast eyes. I'd look to my mother before offering to help cut his meat, but she'd quietly shake her head, no. It seemed doom was on the horizon for my father's business.

Then he came home one day, still in his lab coat, with a giddy grin. He had a massive print card in hand. With a flick of the wrist, he set it twirling on the kitchen counter. My mother stopped the card to inspect it. The front of the card stated in brash golden letters WINNER!!!

"What did we win?"

My father exclaimed, "Dinner with Dudley T. Edger and his family! Know what this means?" He slapped the back of his hand against the palm of the other. "Connections! New clientele. A dinner like this could lead to doing bridgework for billionaires."

"Oh, now, let's not get ahead of ourselves." My mother was studying the brightly lit mansion on the back of the card. "You think they'll be serving heavy breasted steaks with sexy potatoes?" She winked at me then looked back at Martin. "You know, like the commercial."

His face was turning beet red.

"Lipsbeard, Oklahoma?" She continued to inspect the card. "That's in the handlebar part of the state. There's nothing out there for miles. Why would anyone have a mansion in the middle of nowhere?"

My father snatched the card from her hand.

"Can't you see a good thing when it's happening?!"

He stormed out of the room.

My mother looked at me.

"Well, it hasn't happened yet."

I smiled back at her.

***

Three weeks later, my father was gulping down a glass of antacid fizz. My mother had put on her best dress, canary yellow with a long-split back. She'd just finished styling her hair, calling the lacquered column atop her head the Tower of Momisa. "My sculptural project for the week," she said with a giggle. Aside from being a third-grade English teacher, she was also a potter, making pitchers, plates, and cups. Her ceramics studio was in the shed behind our house.

The Oldsmobile engine was running. I strutted into the garage, putting on my baggy dinner jacket. My father was helping my mother with her seatbelt. She was tending to her hair. She had to sit just right, stooped with her tower of hair angled over the dashboard, protecting it with both hands. He was griping about the ridiculousness of her hair. She threatened to stay home if he kept it up. I shut the door and buckled into the seat behind my father. On the drive over, he kept wiping the sweat from the fat rolls along the back of his neck with a handkerchief.

"It's only a dinner," my mother kept saying.

But he was cramped over the wheel, backed up with anticipation. The gated community was more than an hour's drive northwest of Sewell. The flatland consisted of prairie grass and the occasional minor hill. The last several miles ran alongside the Bundy River, the bank walls steep in sections, cobbled with red clay. Next to the entry gate was a stunted and anguished pine tree. My mother was able to catch a glimpse of the sickly tree and the foreboding gate.

"Looks like paradise," she said. "Or a Lipsbeard prison."

"Not funny," my father said. "I'd appreciate some support, not sarcasm."

"You're right," my mother said. "I'm sorry, dear." Then she winked back at me and we shared a private smile.

The entry gate required a code and my father had to wriggle his way half out of the Oldsmobile window. Still it was a strain for him to reach the numerical pad. He was reading the code from the invitation card in his hand. Then he was grappling for the card as a boorish wind sucked it up into the sky like a kite without a string. The same wind pushed at the entry gate and it creaked open a couple of feet. My father told me to go and open it all the way.

When I returned to the Oldsmobile, my mother was still straining at the neck to keep her tower of hair angled just right over the dashboard. Carefully, she turned her head to catch a sidewise view as we started passing one mansion after the other. None of them looked occupied. Like mansions you'd see on a movie set. Great exteriors hollowed out from the inside.

"Are you sure this is the right place?" she said. "Looks like we've entered a graveyard of mansions."

"Well the code worked, of course it's the right place," my father said, but you could see the doubt looming on his face. We'd already gone down one wrong lane to go back up another, and the road before us was growing thin, from two lanes to one lane to a third of a lane. He was struggling to keep the driver-side wheels on the road. It was almost like we were driving on a pedestrian or bicycle pathway—because we were! That's when the tension snapped from his neck and he became a bobblehead of laughter.

This was something he'd been practicing the entire week, at the breakfast table, in the shower, even while tying his shoes. He'd picked up a mass-market paperback on mastering the social graces of conversing with aristocrats and the *nouveau riche*. There was an entire chapter on laughter. How critical it was to perfect the art of laughing with your host, and not seemingly at your host. But the more he strived for authenticity, the more strained his laughter became. Even as we pulled back onto the main road, his laughter was weirdly jovial, a controlled hysteria that shuddered all the way down into his shoes. My mother's hold hardened along the length of her hair.

"The tower's going to crack, Martin, if you keep tapping the brakes like that!"

They'd both been so self-obsessed with their own appearances neither of them had noticed the stain on my white dinner jacket. My mother gasped when she saw it as we stepped out of the Oldsmobile. Then my father saw it, too, and looked away, disgusted.

"Just leave your jacket in the car," he said. He was already halfway up to the palatial front door of the mansion when my mother saw the stain on my shirt. She stopped massaging the back of her neck to hold me in place, with her arms outright and her hands planted on my shoulders.

"What did you do?" She was stunned by the sight of yet another stain. "Paint yourself with gravy on the way out the door?"

"Something like that," I said.

"Why?"

"Why did you make your hair so silly?"

"My hair's not silly!" Gingerly, she touched it, then narrowed her eyes down at me. "What's with the attitude? Is there something I don't know? Are you trying to ruin this night for your father?"

I stared up at her like she might be onto something.

"Know what?" she said. "Doesn't matter. Just cover it up."

And I did, pressing my hand against it, with a smug smile. Truth was this was payback for my father scolding me earlier in the week. Something I'm not sure she knew about. I never told her, and assumed he hadn't told her either. I won't say I wanted to ruin the night for him, but I did want him to know how deeply I could embarrass him at any given moment.

I'll admit I deserved a good scolding earlier in the week, but he'd taken it too far. I can't say what I'd been thinking when I meandered into our basement that afternoon. There was a dental dummy head mounted on an antiquated patient's chair next to the ping-pong table. An old sticky rubber head with a pliable mouth and strong magnetic teeth. Maybe I thought I could learn a dental trick or two to help my father with his business and the declining state of his hand. You know, to be there for him whenever his right hand failed. I was only eleven years old. The things we think when we're kids. I adjusted the chair and the dental dummy head to my height and got to work performing a third-molar extraction. I pulled and pulled and pulled—a white-hot intensity blinding over me. Then everything snapped and I reeled back against a storage rack. Boxes fell, clobbering me on the head. That stubborn molar was still in the dummy's mouth. The next thing I remember was picking up a hammer and marching up to the dummy. After the third whack to the head, to smash that tooth free of his mouth, I suddenly found myself being whisked up into the air. How the ball joint didn't pop from my shoulder socket I'm not sure, but that was how fast my father had jerked me upright by my wrist. The hammer clanked to the floor. He'd never been violent with me like that, and when he released me he was looking at me like I was a murderer. All I had wanted to do was to help. Then he told me to leave and as I sauntered up the stairs, rubbing my shoulder and then my wrist, I could hear him whimpering as he cradled the rubber head in his arms. That dummy head was more important to him than me.

Now we were all standing before the palatial front door of Dudley T. Edger's mansion, and it was oddly quiet. My mother asked again with a hushed tone if we were on time. My father insisted we were, though we no longer had the invitation. Then he reached for the knocker and pulled the brass head of the lion right off the door. He stared at it for a stunned second then tossed it behind the hedges. My mother whispered harshly for me to jump down to retrieve it.

"Why me?!"

That's when the door swung open and we put on our best smiles. It was overwhelming at first, the gaudy and bright entryway of the mansion. My mother braced her tower of hair as she leaned back to gawk up at the chandelier as if seeing the face of God. But if you stared at it long enough you'd sense something fake about that chandelier. I'm guessing it was made of acrylic diamonds with a dollar-store sparkle, and Mr. Edger seemed a lot thinner and older than he did on TV, more bony than plump in his cash-green suit, the skin sagging from his jowls like overcooked roast beef. It was easy to see the scalp netting along the hairline of his stark white wig. Then there was Mrs. Edger in a slender and stunning dress, blue sequins sparkling from her shoulder straps down to her high heels.

There was no mention of the missing knocker as Mr. Edger closed the door, muttering about their butler being on sick leave due to a rare tropical disease contracted during their trip to the Dinkman Islands—a wasting disease that, judging from the gaunt and haggard features of Mr. Edger, he seemed to have contracted as well. My parents were too thrilled to be in the mansion to take note of his muttered aside. They greeted him and his wife with emphatic handshakes.

Then from the distance, beside a large houseplant whose leaves and stalks had been spray-painted gold, a well-groomed rug sprouted stumpy legs and started yapping at us as it rushed over. It was such an angry little face tucked into a bodied rump of woolen hair. Or was it frightened? Mrs. Edger swept the Pekinese dog up into the crook of her arm, where it continued to glare at us with disapproving eyes.

Then my gaze gravitated toward Mrs. Edger's hand. She was missing two fingers, a pinch of scar tissue welted over the base of each knuckle where her pinky and ring finger had once been. Then I saw she was looking at me with her thickly mascaraed eyes. Busted, I looked to the checker-board floor. Her accent was frigid and sharp, Eastern European.

"I know, is not polite to stare."

My mother had seen me staring, too, and started apologizing on my behalf. But Mrs. Edger wasn't accusing me of staring at her hand. In fact, she was accusing *herself* of staring at *my* hand, which I continued to keep pressed against the side of my stomach.

Now everyone was looking at me. The suspicion in my father's eyes flared when he saw the trepidation on my mother's face. He knew what I had was a grenade pin to another stain. But I wasn't ready to blow things up, not yet, so I increased the pressure against the stain, wincing as I announced swimming cramps from practice earlier in the day. "Too many flips and turns along the five-hundred-yard crawl, I s'pose."

My father instantly lightened, gently mussing my hair. "Guess he doesn't know when to quit."

Mr. Edger matched my father's grin with a porcelain show of denture whites. "One of the true signs of an overachiever."

I smiled up at my father.

"Hear that dad? I'm an overachiever."

"Of course you are," he smiled back down at me like *don't blow it, kid.* That's when Mr. Edger clapped him on the back and the cordial round of combustible laughter began with my father giving it his best, "Key-ya-ha-ha-ha!"

And the compliments continued, first with Mrs. Edger admiring my mother's hair, then with Mr. Edger surprising my father by having seen his fifteen-second commercial.

"My commercial?" My father blushed. "What about your commercial? *Bella Mi Fanghi.* Now that's a masterpiece."

Mr. Edger waved a dismissive hand. "Ahhh, way too much production, screams of desperation," he said. "I like your approach. What you have is much more genuine." Then his eyes gunned toward my mother as he slicked the upper bridge of his teeth with the livered tip of his tongue. She was too busy divulging the styling technique of her hair with Mrs. Edger to notice. But my father had caught the lascivious grin and repositioned himself to block Mr. Edger's view of my mother.

"I'm still surprised you've actually seen my commercial."

"Seen it? Oh, come now..." Mr. Edger looked mildly shocked, quoting the tagline. "*All good things in life start with a smile. Make sure yours is the best.*" He waggled a finger at my father. "You come up with that?"

"Well," my father shrugged.

"OK, OK." Mr. Edger clapped him on the back. "Magicians never tell." Then Mr. Edger looked as if he'd swallowed a bug, distancing himself a couple of feet to cough into his hand. After he cleared the phlegm clot from his throat onto a monogrammed hanky, he insisted next on blue Hawaiian cocktails and smoked maple bourbon in the drawing room. My mother and I exchanged one last glance for good luck. We were going our separate ways. My father told me to be on my best behavior. Then they left me with the Edgers' daughter, who'd been watching us from one of the hallway entries.

She'd been standing there with a crocodile-green sweater draped over her shoulders, the sleeves loosely tied over the chest of her cream-colored button-down shirt. Her name was Tabitha. She was pale-skinned and a head taller than me, with razor-thin eyebrows. Her stark bob of blonde hair swerved over her ears to the midpoint of her cheekbones. She was muscular, too, pronounced biceps showing from her short sleeves. Here was someone who could play badminton with a softball. There was a vibratory quiver in her eyes. One that sharpened when she said, "Follow me."

***

In the first room we entered, the ceiling was at least two-stories high. The walls, gilded with decorative trim, featured a series of oil-cracked paintings, arid landscapes with overheated trees. We stopped in front of a pedestal fountain, topped with a concrete cherub freely urinating into a clam-shell pool. She asked about my father being a dentist. I didn't care for her condescending tone, like she was two grades older than me, which she was.

"And how about you?" she said. "Are you planning one day to be a dentist?"

"Planning?" I was glaring at the fat-faced cherub. "Give me a pair of molar forceps and I'll yank the teeth out of that cherub's mouth."

Tabitha winced and was soon tearing up as if what I'd said had pushed her into a puddle of sorrow. *Good*, I thought, as if I'd kicked her on the shin. Then a look of determination hardened over her face. She told me to follow her down another hall. As we trotted along, she wanted to know more about me, and when I told her about my school she shuddered to a standstill as if she'd stepped on a turd.

"Public school, that must be so dreary."

We were both panting as I tried to explain otherwise, adding that my mother was a third-grade English teacher at an awarded public school.

"Warts," Tabitha said.

"Awarded," I said.

"Warts—that's what awards are—warts," Tabitha said defiantly. "Now say warts like ten times really, really fast. You'll see what I mean."

But I didn't and she went on about the awarded warts of her school, East Pampi, a private school next to Rawson's Winery in Watonga, with an annual tuition more than my father makes in three years. She was toying with the sleeves of her crocodile green sweater, telling me how she'd overheard my boasting about swimming cramps. She was also a swimmer and soon concluded I was not, after gathering more specifics about my swim team and practice. Then she left me to stand there alone, singing to herself, "fa-la-la-la-la" down the hall after calling me a liar.

What a snob! I thought, *Thinks she's so special.* A silver-medal triathlete who knows how to conjugate her verbs in French and Italian. Now I was having to sprint to keep up with her. I wanted to yank her by the beltline. Then oomph! I slammed up against her backside. She'd come to a sudden halt, and whisked around unfazed. My nose still burned, zingers of starlight floating inside my eyeballs.

She was mumbling to herself, how everyone over the age of seventeen was an idiot. Then she slapped the wall and I had to triple blink through the fading zingers to see if what I was seeing was actually real, and it *was* real: where she had slapped the wall a rosy imprint of her hand had flushed to the surface as if she'd spanked a bare bottom. Could these walls be alive? The question shuddered through me as I turned to the windows along the hallway. I looked out onto all the other mansions. It was an eerie view, those unoccupied mansions, all of them with a starved vacancy behind every window. The only light paling over the glum scene came from the gibbous moon, nestled in a rip of clouds.

"Idiots," she said again. "That's what they are."

She fell less than an inch to lean back against the wall, which seemed to partially conform to the hold of her shoulders. Then she sighed, inspecting a ball of lint she'd pulled from her sweater sleeve. She stuck it to the wall where it vanished like a pea in mushroom soup.

"Everyone's always lying." She was looking at me now with a mischievous smile. "And your lying about swimming cramps. That was good." She wanted to know if my father was really a dentist. I said that was true. Then she looked at my hand where it was still pressed against my shirt.

"So, if you really don't have cramps then what do you have?" She wanted to see, reaching with a playful hand, but I wouldn't let her.

"Is it a wound?"

"No."

"Then what?"

She sought to corner me as I shifted around her, back-strutting down the middle of the hall.

"It's a mark of triumph," I said and her eyes widened with delight as I peeled back my hand. It was glorious to see, muddied on my shirt, the hideous stain.

"Oh, you feral boy," she said.

Then I recalled with sweet pleasure the moment I had peeled back the lid to that Tupperware container to dredge my fingertips through the congealed gravy to create this stain.

"I did it in protest of tonight," I said, "knowing it would peeve my parents."

"Of course you did." Her smile brightened. "And did it?"

"Let's just say my mother's face buckled when she saw the stain."

"Ha!" Tabitha raised her fist, and I felt elated until she whisked back around, her fierce eyes driving into mine. "But then your mother must have told you to hide that stain and you *did*. See, if you'd been true in protest, a triumph as you say, you would have marched into our mansion boasting of your gravy stain."

Oh, how I hated her all over again. Then she brightened with a wily smile.

"But I have something for that," she said with a telling finger. "And when we sit for dinner tonight it will be with triumph in our eyes. The idiots. You'll see."

"What do you mean?"

"Come, come," she said. "We mustn't waste another second."

***

How many halls could there be? We hadn't even taken a flight of stairs yet. These halls within halls. Each one darker than the last, the lighting becoming murkier with every turn, and yet I felt at ease jogging beside Tabitha, wanting to know more about her and her family. I asked about her mother's mutilated hand.

"You mean my stepmother," she said, adding that Mrs. Edger was her fourth step-mother, a mail-order bride.

"Mail-order?"

"Yes."

Tabitha sprinted ahead.

I shouted after her.

"Why is she missing two fingers?"

"She's a discount bride."

The next corner threw us into absolute darkness. I was reaching with my hands to see, soon feeling the sweater draped over her shoulder. She was waiting for me to look where she'd just signaled with the tilt of her chin. My eyes slowly adjusted to the dull metal square lodged in the wall. Then she pressed a button and it slowly screeched open, a dumbwaiter elevator. She told me to get inside. I looked at her confused.

"But it's an elevator for food and boxes—"

"And boys." Her grin was wide enough to reveal the enamel gleam of a canine incisor. She promised the ride would be *très magnifique*. Reluctantly, I clambered into the small freight elevator. It was a tight fit, requiring me to fold my legs up against my chest and to wedge my head between my knees. The elevator smelled like cabbage farts and bologna sweat. Was she sending me to the garbage room? Then the door scraped to a close and she shouted after me. "Be bold. Be glad. Wherever you descend. Multitude. Solitude."

Her voice faded down the shaft, and soon the cabling jerked to a standstill. Had it been one flight, or two flights down? The door wasn't opening. Was this a trap? Was I stuck between floors? I tried shouting, but my face was crammed too tightly between my knees. Had she led other boys to other dumbwaiters throughout this mansion? Boxing them up to die. I started hyperventilating and could see them in my mind's eye, plotted throughout the various walls of this creepy mansion, like insects fossilized in amber cubes, some shriveled and gray in little-boy dinner jackets, others gangrenous with sunken faces pitted with scorn from having been tricked.

Then the pulley system groaned back into action. Please! I wanted out of this thing. But something else had powered up too. I could hear it from deep within the shaft, a mechanistic and sharp swirling sound. The elevator was plummeting now, my heart beating in my mouth. Death fluttered all around me like batwing skulls maniacal with laughter. The drop speed gaining toward annihilation. There was nothing to do but silently scream. Then with a jolt the ride ended and the door slammed open and I tumbled into a summersault of red light, landing on the floor, helpless as a newborn in a slop of amniotic fluid.

Then I don't know what, a minute, an hour, a day passed. I was still sucking on my thumb, lying before the laces laddered up the shins of Tabitha's field boots. When I finally looked to where she was towering over me, she was backlit by the achingly bright red lighting of the room, a stark silhouette. I ignored the reach of her helping hand as she apologized. I struggled to stand on my own. I wiped the grit and sweat from my palms across the thighs of my pants. Gently, I patted about my rear end, grateful I hadn't crapped myself.

"That was horrifying." I continued looking around the room. "What is this place?"

The room was a cube—the walls, ceiling, and floor glossy latex red. There were only two entrances. A medieval stairwell to the right, ascending into a cavernous hold, and the dumbwaiter behind me. This red lair was a dead end, stinking foul as a barnyard floor heavily misted with Lysol. Tabitha was still standing before me. Behind her was a stainless-steel table supporting a large crate concealed by a gray wool blanket. Was this a slaughter room? Or some sort of kinky dungeon? There were no manacles, or steely instruments of sexual torture hanging about. There was a yellow industrial hose coiled on the wall, and a drainage spout wider than a dinner plate under the table, so my thinking was leaning toward slaughter room.

"I didn't know if I should bring you here, or... " Tabitha looked toward the dumbwaiter. "I should have let you go all the way down."

I looked back at the elevator.

"Where does it go?"

She was twisting at her thumb as if unscrewing a cork. I thought about the whirring sound deep in the shaft that had sounded like a massive meat grinder. My eyes hardened over her. "You were going to send me there?"

"No," she said as if she'd slapped herself. "Well, maybe, yes." She looked back at me imploringly. "But I didn't." She walked up to the crate bed on the table. "This! This is why I brought you here."

She pulled back the blanket. I looked inside the cage. I wasn't sure what I was seeing. Was it a body part? Or some living thing? I leaned in close. It looked like a human torso on a strewn bed of hay. The flesh was almost reptilian with leathery muscled pecs and copper-brown nipples, its barrel-chested body glistening a ruddy golden sheen. Had this once been part of a man? Or was it some sort of mutant creature? There didn't appear to be any genitalia. My mouth was dry, my breathing shallow. There were two bone screws protruding from the meat of its body, the flesh lipped over its collarbone, a gaping dark hollow. Had it been gutted? Or was it some sort of mouth, where a neck should be? A bead of sweat trickled down my spine. I didn't want anything to do with this hideous thing. I glanced over at the steps leading up and out of the room. Tabitha was still staring at me without expression. Then I looked back at the crate bed.

"What *is* that thing?" I said.

We were both staring at it.

"Cruelty," she said.

Her smile was odd, a dimple in her cheek. I couldn't tell if her answer had been one of perverse delight, or sympathy. Then the torso shuddered. I turned to flee. Tabitha stopped me with an overwhelming embrace. Soon I relaxed into her hold, resting the side of my face against her chest. I could smell the warmth of her skin beneath her button-down shirt, like chamomile tea steeped in a stale sweat, and when I pushed away, not to run, but to be there with both her and that... that thing in the crate, she sniffled, clearing a tear from her eye with a swipe of her hand. It was as if the torso had shuddered from its slumber and was now conscious of our being there. That's when she told me his name, which I thought at first was "Him," the pronoun—until she told me it was "Hymn," as in a song of praise.

"In fact," she said with her eyes lighting up as she threaded her fingers through the wire-lattice of the crate. "It was his song that lured me to him in the night."

"What do you mean? Was he something you found? Like in the woods?"

"No, Hymn is from Venezuela."

"Venezuela?!"

"He's not the first one either. Also, mail-order. My father has one delivered every month."

"What?! What for?"

She withdrew from the crate to look back at the elevator. I thought again of that horrible hungry sound from within the pit of the shaft. She said, "There are many rooms in this mansion. And they don't just make themselves. This mansion... it needs to be fed to make new rooms. Rooms that grow, like fat builds on a body."

"Fat? Rooms?" So this mansion *was* a living thing. I started clenching my hands, wringing my fingers.

"Yes, rooms. More rooms than my father could ever possibly need. Rooms without doors, with no one there and no one allowed there except for my father. Now he doesn't know I know *any* of this. All he knows, the idiot, is that he can walk into any room he wants. Even when there are doors."

That's when Hymn started to shriek like a speared dolphin. I thought my brain would shatter. My vision was splitting. There were two Tabithas. Two crates. The red rubbery room was vibrating all over. I clamped my hands over my ears. Quickly, she opened the crate door to soothe Hymn, first by placing a hand over his heart, then by singing *Frère Jacques*. I wondered if Hymn could understand the words. Either way, anyone could understand the tone of a lullaby. Hymn appeared to be growing calm, the contracted muscles of his belly loosening.

Then Tabitha looked back at me, her hand still heavy on his heart.

She said, "Will you help me free Hymn?"

"Me?" I pressed a hand to my chest.

Her eyes looked searchingly into mine. "You said you were the son of a dentist, that you could pull the teeth from that cherub, or was that a lie?"

"No, that wasn't a lie. But what does that have to do with freeing Hymn?"

Her hand moved to one of the bone screws pinned to his collarbone and chained to the crate. What was she suggesting? The red light in the room seemed to brighten and turn hazy. Did she think I'd be able to extract those screws? Then pulling into view from the outer darkness of my mind was a surgical light glaring over the dental dummy back home. His mouth cranked wide. There was that rear magnetic molar that wouldn't give. Even after I'd repeatedly whacked his cheek with a hammer. Had Tabitha known that, she would have never brought me here. Then there was my father looking at me like I was a murderer after shouting at me to stay out of the basement. But Tabitha, ignoring the sweat beading on my face, returned from the shadows of the medieval stairwell with a canvas bag of tools.

"Will you help me?"

I must have nodded yes. There were no bolt cutters, but there was a pair of needle nose pliers. I picked them up with a trembling hand. Then I looked over at Hymn, the red light gleaming off the chains and eye screws bolted into his flesh. This wasn't dentistry. It was more important than that. I took a deep breath, tightening my grip on the pliers. I told her to step back. I got to work.

***

No insect sounds, a calm night, the drizzle of a light rain cooling my face. We were heading across a cumbersome field, our bodies shifting darkly through a hip-high swath of prairie grass. She was carrying Hymn in a duffel bag, the strap slung over her shoulder. The dinner bells were still clanging from the mansion. We were beyond late for the first course. We grappled down the side of a red clay bank. The Bundy River was a wide, deep, flowing channel of ruddy water. The evening light glittered on the current. We were standing at the edge of a sandy reef. After we freed Hymn she told me the river was his natural habitat.

I questioned again if Hymn had once been a man. She didn't know, except that when she first discovered him in the red room he'd been in a large bin of gray water near an empty packing crate from Venezuela stamped "freshwater fish". But he must've been amphibious, like a turtle or a frog, capable of living on land as well. I was surprised by his buoyancy, the seeming ease with which he drifted downriver, the prow of his navel breaching the waves as the stern of his collarbone mouth acted as a motor, gargling up a harmonious drone, pleased to be in his element. Hymn spun around, giving us a nod of the navel while clicking like a dolphin before sputtering on. Our task complete, Tabitha and I shared a triumphant look. We had set Hymn free.

And I felt I had made a new friend, the two of us meandering back through the tall grass, often glancing at each other, brimming with the smiles of co-conspirators. She even took my hand those last few skips back to the mansion.

My parents were waiting for me at the Oldsmobile, demanding to know where I'd been. I could see they'd made it as far as sitting for dinner. There was a bread roll lock-clawed in my father's hand. My mother's tower of hair had cracked, too, no longer a fragile feature atop her head, but scalloped shards of hair that had spilled down the sides of her shoulders. She appeared astonished and somewhat bemused as we settled into the car. I snapped into my seatbelt and looked back at the mansion to wave goodbye. Tabitha was gone.

My father slammed the glove box shut. He'd grabbed the lint roller and was using the handle of it like a knife. "The wretch," he kept calling Mr. Edger as he repeatedly stabbed at the bread roll. Bits of bread spat from his claw. My mother seemed both flattered and mildly disgusted, as if she'd had a forkful of salad slathered with crude oil dressing, after having been invited on a personal tour of Mr. Edger's bed chamber. I won't say that's what happened, but I'd soon learn it was something like that. My father was breathing heavily now. He pulled the lint roller from his hand, slapped it back into the glove box. Maybe he thought my grin in the rear-view mirror was defiant, like *who's the one looking like a murderer now*, but really what I was grinning about was my adventure with Tabitha and having set Hymn free. Then I thought about the dumbwaiter and the whirring sound of blades and how Mr. Edger puts an order in every month for another Hymn. The measure of our heroic act against such a reality was suddenly dwarfed. How many mansions across the globe required such a monthly feast? It was a howling red throat, seemingly infinite, a gluttonous appetite that would never be fulfilled. But we had saved Hymn, and I decided to keep my mind on that, and that alone, and from that righteous place, there was reason enough to see beyond the darkness swiftly moving past the Oldsmobile—something to be proud of.

I thought someday I might see Tabitha again, and I did, almost thirty years later. I saw her name and picture on the local news. She was the owner and CEO of Edger Wind. It seemed Edger Oil had dropped out of the oil business to become a wind-power company. I was an immediate fan, no pun intended, though thankful those wind turbines weren't in my backyard. That's what the news had been about, complaints from a rural community living next to one of the wind farms. The turbines during a strong wind could end up sounding as loud as an airport runway. It seemed an issue Edger Wind was eager to resolve, with a generous settlement for the disgruntled to relocate elsewhere. Then it would be out of sight, out of mind, let the wind blow, as the wind had blown after that night at Edger mansion. In all the years since, I had rarely ever thought about Hymn again.

I did do a cryptid search online once, wondering how such a creature had come to exist, finding a curio on an unsecure website—some fake news you sensed was real—about a South American genetic lab known for unspeakable experiments, gene splicing samples from indigenous peoples with amphibians, reptiles, insects even, somehow related to jungle lore about bug-eyed humanoids with man-sized locust wings. But these days with CRISPR you've got hillbilly Dr. Moreaus working out of their garages, splicing glow-worm DNA with dog semen as if the world would be a better place with a Rottweiler glowing atomic green in the dark. Evolution—it's happening whether we like it or not.

Just last week at Liberty Lake, my friend Carlton reeled in a ten-pound sunfish with human teeth. He even called me over to his place to confirm the fact out on the rear deck of his house. The short hairs stiffened up my arms as I pried opened its mouth. I still get chills thinking about those wonky teeth and that gray gum-line crowded with molars. Then we drank beers over the toothy mutant and I thought to tell him about Hymn. But I'd never told anyone about Hymn, so I swallowed the thought with the next sip, which went down the wrong pipe. Carlton asked if I was okay after I'd coughed myself red in the face. I assured him I was, continuing to stare at the toothy sunfish on the table.

There was still a bit of curiosity itching at the back of my neck after seeing Tabitha on the nightly news, so the following day after work I decided to take the long drive home, one that would have me passing through Lipsbeard.

I'd become a podiatrist's assistant at the Foot-and-Ankle center on Colfax Avenue. I was still in my blue scrubs, waiting for the last traffic light out of town to change. My right hand was bandaged from an accidental burn earlier in the day. I'd seared it against a steam sanitizer, causing a mess. I could still hear the metal instruments falling from the tray, a clank of bone cutters, nail splitters, and moon-head nippers. But that didn't stop my fingers from dancing on the steering wheel of my Toyota Prius on that drive out into the prairie. A golden oldie crooning on satellite radio, "16 Candles" by Johnny Maestro and The Crests.

Dusk was more gray than red—like a grim curtain over the prairie. Then I saw them to my right, the wind turbines out on the horizon. I pulled over to the side of the road to walk down to the Bundy River. It was easy to see across the current where the mansions had once been. All gone now. I saluted those distant turbines, a colony of towering poles capped with slow twirling blades.

If you google Mr. Edger's name you'll quickly see the

foreclosures, scandal, scandal, scandal, bankruptcy and federal indictment, and then bye-bye Mr. Edger. When his financial ruin played out on prime-time news my father and I shared a laugh over the phone. True laughter, unlike the staged laughter he had worked so hard to produce that night at Edger mansion. My mother was laughing too, and though it was a long-distance call from Arizona, where they had retired after twenty-five years in business together—Forever Smile: boutique porcelain veneers, crafted by my mother with surgical precision, installed by my father with a gentle touch—the signal was clear enough to feel that we were all in the same room. I skipped a flat stone across a placid stretch of the Bundy River. A series of concentric circles rippled one after the other. I cupped my hands to my mouth to blow between my thumbs, and even with a bandaged hand was able to produce the quivering notes of a mourning dove. I even sang a couple of lines: *Frère Jacques, dormez-vous, ding, dang, dong.* Not that a poorly rendered lullaby would attract a response, but you never know. The trickling of the current was friendly. In tone.

AFTER THE RIDES

We took the shuttle to the entrance of the theme park. My father said, Remember our car is in Squiggly section C.

The day was thrilling.

When we returned to Squiggly section C, there was another family inside our car. They looked just like our family. My father stopped my mother and me from yelling at them as they drove away.

We sat in the empty parking space. Many families came and went. None of them noticed us. A girl from one of the families stepped on my hand without acknowledging me. Eventually the parking lot was empty. The theme park tower lights shut down. We were exhausted and hungry.

In the middle of the night, Father woke us up. The shuttle had returned. The driver had no face. There was another groggy-eyed family on the shuttle. They too were identical to our family. We stepped inside the shuttle and introduced ourselves, but they said nothing, ignored our presence, and held each other close. We drove on.

My father nudged me on the shoulder. I had fallen

asleep. It was morning and the shuttle had pulled up in front of our house. We were home. The other family had already gotten off the shuttle. We followed them to the front door. Our car was in the driveway and the family that had stolen our car was watching us from the living room window.

Our family and the family from the shuttle stood in line and, one at a time, we knocked on the front door. Nobody answered. My father and the other father said they would be right back. They disappeared behind the house. My mother and the other mother did not talk to each other. I stared at the other boy. He was growling at me. Then the front door opened. I could not tell which of the three fathers staring back at us was mine. We all went inside.

Everyone sat in the living room. One of the fathers spoke first. He said by the end of the day there would only be one family. The other two fathers nodded. I felt queasy and confused.

So how do we determine which family stays, one of the mothers said.

We have a contest, one of the boys replied.

That's right, the three fathers said. One of the fathers looked at me. I had wet myself and soon everyone was looking at me. The other boy pointed, Does that mean he goes first?

No, no, the three mothers blurted. None of the boys can go first.

I was crying and the words trembled from my lips, Go where?

One of the fathers stood up and said, I will make this easy. He marched into the study and we all heard the gun. He had shot himself dead. None of the mothers seemed to mind, nor did the other two boys. The two living fathers dragged the body down into the basement.

One of the boys grabbed my hand. Wanna play outside? I snatched back my hand and rushed to my room and slammed the door and tried to lock it, but the lock had been removed. I pushed against the door, but they bullied their way into the room. One was tugging at my hair and the other was pulling at my legs. Take off his shoes! Take off his pants! See, he's still wet with pee. I was kicking and kicked myself free then whirled around and wrestled the other boy to the floor, and then I felt myself getting lifted into the air.

One of the fathers carried me into the study and placed me onto his leather chair. He left me there alone. I hugged myself and rocked back and forth while everyone whispered outside the closed door. There was a chunk of brain matter on the family portrait from the first father who had shot himself in the mouth. The boy in the portrait was wearing a blue dress and his hair was in pigtails. The study door opened. The two boys entered first, followed by the three mothers and two fathers. The herd of parents goaded the boys to apologize, and I accepted.

Then everyone stared at one another and the pendulum inside the grandfather clock halted into a mid-swing silence that loomed all around.

Let's play Twister, one of the mothers said.

I felt uncomfortable in urine-soaked pants and asked if I could change. Then I noticed the other two boys had wet their pants too. Don't worry about it, the three mothers said. Today's our last day. Live it like it's your first.

I don't know about you, but seeing your parents strip naked can be very uncomfortable.

My three wives, one of the fathers joked as the other father stoked the flames in the fireplace. The sky was evening blue and the fire crackled and our bodies were tiger orange except for the faces in the shadows. The Twister board was on the floor in front of the fireplace.

Twenty-three colored dots were on the board. Seven were black holes. The trick is to keep all your body parts. Boys, have a seat. The two fathers sat as well. The dial on the color wheel twirled. We watched the mothers play Twister on the floor. They contorted in and around each other like human pretzels. Every time the spin dial pointed to a black hole one of the mothers lost a limb.

The lost limb reappeared on the side of the playing board. The fathers leaned forward from their wing-back chairs to pick up the arm or leg for examination before passing it on to us. I held one of my mother's legs and recognized the mole on the inside of her left thigh. It felt good to trace my fingertip up and down the length of her leg. Her toes bunched as I tickled the bottom of her foot. Soon the other two boys were wrestling for possession over the remaining three torsos writhing on the Twister board. The boys simultaneously shoved each other into two separate black holes. The house rumbled as if painfully swallowing something too large for its throat. The boys never reappeared. Their fading screams shuddered over me. I was the only boy left. The two fathers were sitting by the fire, sharing a cigar. The flames dancing in the fireplace blurred out of focus. My eyelids were falling, heavy with sleep.

I woke up and the house windows welcomed the morning sun. The Twister board was gone. I was the only one left in the living room. A hunchbacked cleaning woman was vacuuming the floor. The sound of crushed potato chips tinkled up the metal pipe. The air stank of Father's cigar. When I walked past the cleaning woman she grunted at the floor like, I'm not cleaning that up.

She was talking about one of the fathers. He was half-inflated, his legs rolled up to his ribs on the wooden floor. The instructions on how to package the inflatable father were on the dining room table. There was still enough air in his head to make a puffy show of lips, like the lips of a father ready to blow a heart-shaped ring of smoke.

I stepped over him. I was hungry. I would pack him up later. There was a note on the kitchen counter. I waited until after eating a bowl of cereal to read it.

I trust you slept well. I'll be in the study whenever you're ready. Love, Dad.

There was a blonde wig with pigtails on the kitchen counter. The cleaning woman asked what she should do with the human hand she had found under the sofa.

I told her I'd take care of it. It was my mother's hand. The hunchback grunted then continued vacuuming. I took the wedding band off my mother's finger and wore it as my own. Then I pulled the pigtail wig tight onto my head. I knew Daddy would be pleased to see his little girl. Quietly, with my mother's hand, I opened the study door.

THE PLACENTA TREE

The tip of the trowel broke dirt. Roots thumped. May stabbed again.

"Be sure you work it in a circle," the woman said.

May jabbed out an oblong circle.

"Now dig out the dirt," the woman said.

May thrust her hands into the earth. The woman smiled. May tossed dirt to the side. She came across a root and tugged. It wouldn't budge. She wedged the trowel underneath and pulled. She grunted. The root snapped. Dirt jumped into her face. She turned and spat and brushed the dirt from her mouth. She dug some more.

"That's good," the woman said.

May stood and clapped her hands clean.

The woman crouched before the pit. The red bandana tied to her head fluttered open, revealing her bald head. Her eyes were sore, redlined and pink. She squinted at the hole in the ground as if it was a painful thing to see, the black soil and damp roots.

"Now get my knapsack," she said.

At the trunk of a high-rising tree, May grabbed the

knapsack by the strap and dragged it along the ground, parting dead leaves.

"Don't drag it," the woman said.

May lifted the strap and laid it across her forehead. The sack bounced off her butt as she traipsed along. She stopped beside the woman. They gazed into the dark hole.

The woman took the knapsack and flopped open the flap. She pulled out a large Tupperware container. There was something dark inside. She pulled the lid off. A rank metallic odor struck the air. Inside the container was a maroon blob covered with tufts of frost. Placenta. It had been stored in the freezer since May had been born. The woman wanted to save it for the right time, a time that May would remember. She set the container beside the pit.

"All right," she said.

May kneeled beside her. Together they lifted the back end of the container. The placenta slipped over the edge, thick and thin vascular stretches, and slopped into the hole. Then their hands, young and old, bulldozed the mounds of excavated dirt until the placenta was a black blob in a shallow pit of soil.

"Now get the sapling," the woman said.

By the same poplar tree, May grabbed the sapling. Baby leaves fluttered as she trotted back to the pit, smiling. Her milky white teeth gleamed. She held up the baby tree. A burlap sack was tied to the bottom. The woman untied the twine, pulling the sack from the bottom of the sapling, revealing a clump of dirt. May placed the baby tree onto the pit, holding it there while the woman filled the remainder of the hole. Then together on their knees, they spanked the earth, a jumble of hands, leaving large and small imprints on the black soil. The sapling quivered.

They stood and held hands, their arms circled around the sapling. The woman looked at May and nodded. They closed their eyes. The sunlight was warm against May's face, especially her eyelids, making her warm all over. The wind blew. Leaves rustled. The top flap of the woman's bandana fluttered into a paisley crown, revealing on her bald head a dime-sized tattoo of black dots. Next to the tattoo was a singular hair that swayed upright like a crisp antenna. The woman spoke.

"To you, the incomprehensible fabric of the world formed in a circle. To you, who give through sun, moon, and earth and ask for nothing in return. To you who live in us all, spiraling out through the air to the ether and to the outer stretches of the universe. To you we say..." She squeezed May's hands.

"Greetings," they said in unison.

The bald woman tongued the sores in her mouth, then continued, "And with our greetings we ask that you accept this sapling and its life. We ask that you will help it to grow as you have helped us. And on this day, in this time, this is what we ask. May it be heard."

May giggled.

"Now be with us in silence," the woman said.

A crow cawed in the distance. A cloud eclipsed the sun. May opened her eyes, slightly chilled by the cloud's shadow and the sight of a baby leaf, keeping its hold on the branch as it danced against a gentle wind. The woman was still praying, eyes closed, mouthing silently to some greater beyond.

A strip of flagging tape, hazard red, was tied around the thick wide trunk of a dead oak tree. May was singing when the woman hooked the beltline of tape with her fingers and pulled. It stretched, gummy, then broke. Single-handedly, the woman balled it up and stuffed it into her knapsack. She muttered angrily. May looked up at her. They kept walking through the woods. May continued singing.

"Placenta tree. Placenta tree. We just planted a placenta tree, pla-cen-ta tree... Mommy?"

"Yes, dearie."

"Is the placenta tree going to grow up and have organs like we do?"

"Not exactly," the woman said, smiling.

"Then what?"

"Well... our placenta will disintegrate into the earth and the tree will get its nutrients from that and grow."

"So the tree won't have organs?"

"No."

"Oh," May said, then wondered if the tree would have a brain, not realizing that too was an organ. Even if she did, she wouldn't have asked. They kept walking. May kicked a dead branch. It skidded across the leaves. She bit her lip and looked at her mother's boots flecked with paint—green, black, and gray, some of the dried flecks the color of flesh.

They stopped.

There was a flagged wooden stake hammered in the ground.

"What's that?" May said.

"A property marker," the woman said.

They gathered around the wooden stake.

"Nobody owns this land," the woman muttered, "Nobody." But she knew the land was marked, possibly for construction, possibly for clear-cutting. The woods slowly swirled around her as she kicked the stake, right boot, left boot, until the wooden stake loosened from the ground. She pulled it out. The tip was soiled. She tore the red flagging from the stake and handed the stake to May.

"Go bury this under some leaves."

May trotted off.

The woman looked down and in the ground was the dirty white cap of the property marker. She crouched with her knobby knees jutting up and thumbed the dirt from the cap. It read: Grazer & Sons. Cheeks flushed with anger, she clawed around the cap, revealing a steel rod. She clawed out more dirt and latched onto the rod. The muscles in her arms tightened as she pulled, grunting.

"Come on... come on... "

She continued to tug, a spastic jerking, but the steel rod wouldn't budge. Her grip tightened. Yesterday seized her mind. The hospital.

The room is cold and sterile. The blue slipover loosely tied across my back. I feel like the incredible shrinking woman, shrinking in front of the white plastic machine that looks like a gigantic toy faucet. The nurse tells me to lie on the steel table. The feeling is as cold and sterile as the room, the steel pushing flat against the exposed skin of my back, legs, and heels. My heart is racing, but I keep telling myself it's all right. The nurse asks if I'm okay. I nod. Then she puts the thermoplastic mask on my face. I look up at the white plastic ring of the faucet. The x-ray circle. The nurse screws the mask to the table so my face won't move. She leaves.

There are voices on the intercom. I keep my eyes open and still. The room goes dark. The faucet clicks. The x-ray circle lights up, black and grey. I know it's aimed at the dots they tattooed on my head. I feel nothing. The radiation targeting the cancer in my brain. I can't feel it, but I know it's killing everything within its range, the good and the bad.

May could hear her mom in the distance, struggling. She dropped more leaves, spreading them with her foot, burying the wooden stake. Then she looked up and across the way. There was a fawn standing there, its caramel-colored hide spotted with creamy dots. May's eyes widened, excitement beating in her heart, as they studied each other. The fawn's lively black eyes, stained with tears dark as syrup, tilted from view. The fawn pranced through the trees, delicately disappearing. May gasped.

The woman had surrendered. The fight of it all still cramped in her jaw, where she remained crouched round the steel rod. May ran towards her, flailing with excitement.

"I just saw a deer. A baby deer."

The woman looked up, exasperated. She coughed onto the back of her hand, a dry sickly cough.

"You did?"

"Yeah, over there, over there," May pointed. "Over there. Did you see?"

"No," the woman said hoarsely.

"Oh my god, it was so pretty. I've never seen anything like it, the baby deer. You should have seen it, it was so, so deery."

"Well that's nice," the woman said and stood up and brushed the dirt from her hands.

"I wish you'd seen it," the girl said.

The woman looked down at May.

"Well I see you," she said with a loving smile, "that's enough for me."

Distant through the trees, parked alongside a country road, was their green Plymouth station wagon. May took giant steps while the woman walked with a gnarled stick for a cane, jabbing into the earth with every step. May stopped, reared back, and then jumped. She pranced about, getting lighter with each step. She reached for her mother's hand, missing.

"I wonder why the baby deer was alone."

The woman tested a wide patch of mud, poking it with the stick.

"Watch your step," she said.

They walked around the mud.

"Maybe its mother was sick."

"No," the woman said. "The mother wasn't sick."

"How do you know?"

"I just do."

"Oh," May said. She wanted to ask more but stayed silent.

The woman tossed the knapsack into the back of the station wagon. It landed next to a cluttered stack of canvases. The top canvas was an oil painting, a surreal mountain shaped like a brain, its crumpled flesh bountiful with trees and bushes. The skyline was menacing, black and grey, a swirling void.

Still parked on the side of the country road, the woman was in the driver's seat, greedily drinking from a plastic bottle of water. No matter how much she drank, every sip scorched her throat, a raw and throbbing thirst she could not fulfill. May watched her mother with concerned curiosity. The woman finished the bottle, screwed the cap back on, leaving it empty on the bench seat between her and her daughter. The sores in her mouth burned. She winced, tenderly tonguing behind her wisdom tooth. She reached under the seat, pulling out another bottle. Untwisting the white cap, she clenched it as she gulped more water. May sniffled and turned, hiding her face from her mother. Outside the passenger window her view of the distant woods turned bleary. All she wanted was the placenta tree to grow up with a brain, a healthy brain that was forever.

MAN OF THE SAW

Ahhh, the soothing sounds of the Chainsaw Americans. You can hear them, less than a quarter of a mile away, marching up the avenue. Thousands of them, buzzing in unison. Louder than a flock of Harleys. There's only one sound missing from that march and that's the sound of my Vaz Deferenz KR-14.

A stub titanium blade with monster horsepower.

That stump daddy may look like a chump chainsaw, but the speed of the chain and zero-gravity weight makes up for what it lacks in a long-dong of titanium steel. The song of my Vaz Deferenz is a mighty *scree*. One I'll be cranking sooner than later. Generally, I'm not an open-carry kind of guy. That's why I left my Vaz in Harlow's apartment. But soon as I drop him off, I'll crank up the Vaz, grind that stump daddy over my head, join the march, my saw among the many.

I'm a dog walker and Harlow's my last walk of the day, a bulldog with a toothy underbite and a thick-headed strut. I'm cutting his walk short—not proud of it. He seems annoyed too as I drag him past a prime hub for pee mail. I'd have done it regardless. It's insulting. No dog should be allowed to pee on the leg of a mailbox from the United States Postal Service. See how the leg has corroded. Soon it'll be a three-legged mailbox. There should be consequences for such behavior! Laws drafted. Fines enforced and incarceration for repeat offenders, and I'm not talking dogs but their owners and walkers who allow such an act to continue.

Sorry, Harlow. There you will not pee. But the stand of a coin-operated phone? Have at it. Then we pick up the pace, two-and-a-half blocks from dropping Harlow off at his apartment, two-and-a-half blocks from my Vaz waiting for me in its snap-lock case. I can feel the excitement tingling up into my arms.

We're on West 11th Street, Sixth Avenue up ahead. That's where the march is happening, on the Avenue of the Americas.

Listen to them, Harlow.

Marching from downtown, a crank-and-rod choir of saws, Farm Boss to Makita to Craftsman, and if you sharpen your ear you can hear the gentle flourish of Greenwork blades, those lithium go-getters, hedge snippers with Jurassic teeth.

But come on!

The testosterone of a saw doesn't come with an electrical chatter. It comes with the stink of a diesel boost. Something you can trigger. A high-powered extension of the arms. But today, a saw's a saw, even if you have to plug yours into the wall to charge it up. Long as you hold yours over your head during the march, grind that sucker at the air, you'll be one of many. That's the sound of freedom. The hip-hip-hooray of America, a mighty buzz. Makes a man sniffle. Enough to thumb a tear from my eye. Makes me want to sing. Sing with me, Harlow!

Oh, beautiful for gracious saws, from tree to shining tree. Confirm thy soul in self-control. Saw down your fellow trees. Americans. Americans. Brandish your saws for thee.

Oh, man! Feel the boom thunder beneath your feet, the notch-and-carve of felling a virgin tree. Wood pulped into paper, ink on the constitution, men in colonial wigs, scribing our rights. Why, had it not been—

A yank to the arm, a skin burn to the wrist, the leash pulled tight, Harlow is looking at me from where he has slammed on the brakes like, *Get over yourself, dude!*

Then I tug the leash and we're back in action, Harlow reluctantly marching behind me. I can sense through the leash as he continues to pull against my charge that he's stressed by the march of saws. The collective buzzing getting louder. And as we turn onto Sixth Avenue, with a squint I can see them approaching.

I know we should be rushing along, my Vaz only two blocks away. But first, I must salute, waggle my imaginary saw overhead, give it a buzz with clenched teeth, working the sound up from the meat of my throat. This stresses Harlow out even more.

Then I have to assure him. Tell him Chainsaw Americans are not a haphazard crew. There's no tomfoolery. No, sir. There are regulations. Rules of safety to abide by. Don't let the pull of the saw pull you into an accident. You have to respect the saw. Stand tall when you work it. Bend your knees with a boxer's stance. Never, ever power up your saw inside your home, or bedroom, or bathroom. The garage is okay. Know what I'm saying? And I'm not sure Harlow does.

His owners are NPR fanatics. Harlow's always zonked out on the bean bag when I pick him up for his walk, tranquilized on Lakshmi Singh. In fact, Lakshmi was reporting today about a record turnout for today's march. Though she could have been more enthusiastic about it. You'd think someone sawed the legs off her desk. It's not personal, it's electoral. Just how the confetti popped red this past election.

Hey!

I point for Harlow to see. There is a handwritten sign in the restaurant window beneath a dozen hung Peking ducks painted on the glass. Even this Chinese restaurant values the importance of the Chainsaw Americans. See! "10% off for Chainsaw Good People." They know—*they know!*—what we bring to this country. Though why they wrote Chainsaw Good People instead of Chainsaw Americans I'll be sure to ask. Maybe their English is off. But still, seeing that! You know they know what's up with the Chainsaw Americans.

It's not just a tiered system of entitlement either. Like I said, any saw can join; so can any race, religion, creed, or cretin for that matter, even if the beans in the brain are askew, as some might say of me, but hey, long as you're an American! All we need's proof of citizenship, twelve out of the fourteen stated documents: birth certificate, passport, dental records, proof of paying taxes, license to carry a chainsaw. Rest assured, health insurance is not one of the fourteen documents, so don't go sweating that. Then there's the one-in-the-family all-in-the-family clause, which means even you, Harlow, could be a Chainsaw American, if one of your owners joined.

Then we could eat all the Chinese with our chainsaws, 10% off. That didn't sound right, did it? I meant Chinese food like they meant Americans when they scribbled "Good People" on that sign. But there's always more than one way to read something. In fact, some people try to drag the good out of Chainsaw Americans, saying the name implies that's what we want to do! As in chainsaw Americans—to pieces.

Oh man! They're close. Even from the lobby of the Bruegel you can hear them marching up the avenue. We're waiting for an elevator and Harlow's still got the grumps like I jilted him out of his walk. But your owners'll be home soon. That's the frown I give him before I smile with glee, knowing soon I'll be with the saws, thousands of them.

There are some fans outside too. There to greet those Chainsaw Americans. Snap pics. Post live feeds. And sure, some protestors too. Permanent markers scribbled on tree-free poster board. Stop the Chop! Paper-free America! Some nasty ones too. What if I clear cut the Garden of Eden? And to that I'd say there'd be more Bibles. Though I'm not a man of God. I'm a man of the saw. My Vaz Deferenz KR-14 now only an elevator ride away. But worse than gum on your shoe, these elevators are stuck to the shaft. One's out of service. Okay, one's moving up now, going up, up, up, but still there's another one stalled on the 14th floor, which is really the 13th floor.

See, even here superstition follows everyone around. Can't have a 13th floor. No one would live on it. Only there is a 13th floor. They just skipped it, calling it the 14th floor. That's where Harlow lives too, on the 13th floor. Oops, did I just say that out loud? But with Chainsaw Americans there is no superstition. Only the power of the grind. But it does cross my mind that a KR-14 could be a stand-in for KR-13, but like I said, Chainsaw Americans are not superstitious.

Finally, we're at Harlow's apartment and if his owners had lived on the other side of the hallway I'd have an aerial view from their window of the march below.

Let's get this over and done with, Harlow. Scoot. Scoot. Scoot. I close the door behind me because he has this tendency to dart out into the hall. Then I unleash him, give him a wink, grab a Kong from the freezer, his post-walk treat, a bouncy chew toy filled with peanut butter.

But I'm too excited to hand the Kong off to Harlow, leaving it on the dresser beside the front door. All I can do is stare at the carry-case also on the dresser. I unbuckle the snaps. There it is like a sax in the case. My Vaz Deferenz KR-14, my stump daddy, my American right.

Maybe I'll just crank it up a little. Give Harlow a show. I know, I know, I'm breaking one of the cardinal rules of being a Chainsaw American, but today's a special day. I crouch before the saw after setting it on the Persian carpet, holding it in place with my foot. Let's crank this baby up.

And damnit, Harlow!

You have to back off. Seriously. This saw will buzz you in half, quit fooling. I guess I was too excited, leaving his peanut-butter Kong on the dresser. I should have given it to him before yanking the starter cord. But my instinct for the saw is too strong. What we have here, Harlow, is a conflict of interest, as when a man eats first before feeding his dog. Thus, a man of the saw must crank his Vaz before treating Harlow to a Kong.

Oh man! I can already hear the march through the walls and I'm buzzing that stump daddy over my head, *Brrt-Brrt-brreeeeee.*

Who's the boss, Harlow! Who's the boss!

Let's just say this doesn't end well. I could spare you the details. How Harlow charged into my ankle like a bowling ball with teeth. How my hold on the Vaz swung down to my thigh, a gored spray accenting the wall. A supreme act of idiocy, I know. No fault of Harlow's. I should have given him his Kong and now I do, before slumping to the floor, knocking it from the dresser, watching him chase after it as it bounces across the carpet.

Harlow's fine, just some blood spatter to the face, like all he wanted was the Kong, like all I wanted was the Vaz, makes us both creatures of instinct, though I've always considered mine free will, the right to buzz a saw, the right to Friday night boilermakers, the right to jam down on an all you-can-eat breakfast at four a.m. Is this no different than Harlow gnawing and tonguing the peanut butter from his Kong? Absolutely dogged I am with salutations of pride, even with the Vaz still wedged in my leg—wedged enough I fear, that pulling it free would mean another spurt from the deep vein in my thigh. My hands are too slip-sliding bloody to use the phone.

All one can do is sing, right Harlow?

I can hear the march through the door and the outer hall and the doors of the opposing apartments, beyond the outer walls of the Bruegel, thirteen stories below. I can hear them, marching in the thousands, far too loud, far too proud for any call for help to be heard. I warm myself with a consoling hug against the chill shuddering through my bones. Sing with me, Harlow—*Oh, beautiful for gracious saws.*

FUNERALS FOR ANIMALS

It was freeze-your-face cold on the Lower East Side, six p.m. dark, the sidewalks encrusted with dirty snow and salted footpaths, but Nuclear Gene was heating everyone up at the bar with Florida sunshine on his burner phone.

Glitchy low-res pics of palm trees, a flamingo-pink motel, beachgoers out on the sand in speedos and skimpy bikinis. These weren't pics from a trip he'd already taken, but search-engine pics from a trip he was going to take after having scratched up a win on a New York Lotto card less than a half hour ago.

It wasn't millions. It wasn't even 10k. In fact, it was hardly enough for a one-way ticket to a king-sized suite. But the way he kept saying, "Days upon Days in Daytona," you'd think he'd scratched up a lifetime of cash to some farty hot tub in the sky.

What did we care?

The drinks in our hands were compliments of Nuclear Gene, enough to have us all flatly cheering him on like he'd scratched up a big-daddy win. Plus, it was good to see someone on our crew suddenly flush with cash. Like a video-game explosion of gold coins. Miracles can happen. Even when they're small.

We were all still thawing out from another deep freeze on a back-aching shift at a luxury high-rise without heat. There were still over four hundred doors to install, several custom staircases, balustrades, and loft guardrails for various condos and penthouse suites. We were non-union metal workers without worker rights and possibly another week without pay. But you didn't talk about that, unless you were looking for a smackdown from the starved look in everyone's eyes. The superstition being to bring it up might further jinx the prospect of soon getting paid. Everyone knew there were outstanding invoices that, once fulfilled, would trickle into our pockets. You just never knew when. Most of the crew was slumped at the bar, clad as armadillos in skull caps, cadet hats, canvas jackets, padded pants, and work boots.

Of course, we all had passions besides drinking ourselves shitty off the clock. Meathead Jack had his GoPro skater vids. Fonda had her comedy routine, always on the hunt for an open-mic, a lively act about her childhood years with a four-inch tail before having it amputated when she was seven years old. Kenyan John had his dub-trance-electro band *Spleef Nnnrr-Eye*, and Kyra had a screenplay-in-the-works on social injustice. "And no, it isn't about us, though it should be," she once said, "because we're a bunch of dumb asses for working so long without pay."

Nuclear Gene slapped another hundo on the bar and said, "'Nother round on me, fuckos!" That got him another cheer, and more eyes trained on him.

In a flimsy, bejeweled, cardboard Burger King crown, he was still ranting about what he was going to do with all that money. Already looking flame-grilled as Daytona Royalty, his crispy eyebrows dyed as ghoulishly green as the back drape of his hair, he had that burner phone snuggled up to his lips like a rockabilly mic, all breathy and jittery, a rotten show of corn-nut teeth.

"I'm talking a king-sized suite with a balcony view of all the hotties down by the pool, slathering their bronzed arms, legs, and inner thighs, *ooooooweeeee*, with coconut oils and spunk loads of suntan lotion."

Everyone was cracking up, enjoying the show. I gave it a half-smile, time to time. Alone at a corner table, bottled beer in hand, I was scratching at the label, ripping silvered strips of paper. There was a party coming up that Friday at Kyra's loft in Dutch Kills, Queens. Guess you could say my mind was on that.

Kyra was one of two TIG welders on our crew, broad-shouldered, Puerto Rican-Irish mix, always on the job with black stallion gloves. I'd met one of her roommates at another party, a modern dancer named Stacy, and was wondering if she'd be at said party that Friday. I was too shy to ask Kyra, who was currently giving mouth to mouth to a sandy blonde in a busty biker jacket at the end of the bar. I wasn't even sure if Stacy liked guys or not. I'd overheard Kyra talking about her once.

How Stacy had pampered all her loft mates one Sunday, curing their hangovers with a dynamite brunch she'd whipped up, western omelets with hash rounds and mimosas. If Stacy did have a significant other it was a fact I'd fogged over, imagining a hangover cure of my own, the two of us sharing a hair-of-the-dog can of Pabst Blue Ribbon. I was already slurping the foam from a freshly cracked can so she could have the first clean sip.

It was a couple of weeks ago at a Williamsburg loft party where we first met. Nothing more than a five-minute conversation, but more than enough to keep running it through my mind. Funny how a small crush can turn seismic. The party was on the top floor at the Pencil Factory, with an expansive view outside the windows softly out-of-focus, the night lights of the Manhattan skyline reflecting off the East River.

There were microwaved pigs-in-a-blanket with no paper plates. One of the hot snacks escaped my hold and bounced over to her iridescent combat boots. I knew who she was as I walked up to her, but pretended I didn't as I bent over to pick up the little weenie. She asked if I was looking to start a food fight. That got the convo going. Soon we were talking about a Satanic funeral for a house cat in some Kenneth Anger film, which then led to discussing the open casket scene of Norma Desmond's pet chimp in Sunset Boulevard.

I was surprised she knew these cinematic references, as she was at least ten years younger than me. I seem to recall her saying something about an extracurricular class on cinema she'd had in high school at the Chicago Academy for the Arts. That's when she straightened the blue wig on her head and I pretended to suddenly recognize her.

I asked if she'd been part of a collective show at PS1 called *The Body Apocalypse*. She gave a modest smile and I downplayed my enthusiasm. I told her I liked her part of the show, when really her performance had had a profound effect on me. It was staged in absolute darkness, so you couldn't even see her at first. The music was moody, pensive, and mysterious, and when your eyes adjusted, there were frenzied glimpses of flesh, almost nightmarish, yet reverential and fierce. It was so intense that during her performance I'd unknowingly twisted the program into a tight-fisted scroll.

She seemed almost embarrassed by my having seen her show. I said nothing more about it, instead suggesting we look up the name of Norma Desmond's chimp on my phone. The conversation abruptly ended with someone luring her by the wrist deeper into the party. But she did look back as if she could've kept on talking.

I race-walked back to my apartment that night, tried to calm myself with a few poems from Baudelaire's *Flowers of Evil*, but it was too much, the grim snorts, darksome beauty, and sprawling night hills. I slammed the book back into the freezer after grabbing a couple of ice cubes for a stiff drink.

I did eventually get around to looking up the name of the chimp. I won't say I was looking forward to telling her the next time we happened to meet that there wasn't one. At least no evidence of it online. But then maybe that could be a challenge for us. Give our dead chimp a name. I already had a few in mind. Alchemical names like Mercurio, Bismuth, Cinnabar. Something that might incite an occultist smile. I don't know, the whole thing was starting to make me feel nauseous.

My fingertips were sticky from shredding the beer-bottle label into nervous little strips. D.O.A. was crashing out of the jukebox, hardcore punk, *Whatcha Gonna Do?!*

Everyone was still shouting at Nuclear Gene, goading him on. He'd clambered up onto the bar to air-hump on an invisible piece of ass, slapping at it as he flicked his tongue.

I wiped the shreds from the table then placed four fingers to my lips to add to the hoopla with a shrill whistle of enthusiasm. I was all bravado on the outside for Nuclear Gene, but on the inside I was still at the cork board trying to come up with names for some dead chimp... Alowishus, Paternus, DaDa ...

***

Friday. The end of the work week was less than an hour away. That Dutch Kills party was still on the roster. I was finishing another steel door. The Krylon spray sputtered empty and I tossed the can to the floor. A hot shard of sunlight reflected off the high-rise across the street. There'd been news of a freakish warm front on the way. You could sense it from the heat in the late-afternoon streak of sunlight. I pulled the respirator from my nose and mouth. A Krylon mist still clung to the air, sweet as the taste of cotton candy. Too bad huffing the shit won't get you high. Smell it for too long and you'll end up with a migraine.

I looked out at the high-rise across the street. Most of the offices on every floor had cleared out for the weekend. I'd yet to expand upon the potential list of names for Norma Desmond's dead chimp, which was okay, because I didn't want to seem too over-prepared should Stacy be at the party.

It was time for a piss break, that early-afternoon cup of coffee pushing at my bladder. There were still no porta-johns on the nineteenth floor. The closest portas were on the tenth floor, and no way was our crew boss, Anders, going to let us hit those, knowing that the slow-ass construction elevator, or the walk nine flights down, nine flights up was an invitation to a one-to-two-hour piss break.

He'd confronted management about it when we started the job over two months ago, saying we needed portas closer than that. The overall site manager was a thick-necked Serb from Bosnia named Osmos, a welter-weight baldie in a cherry hard hat; his nose was crooked with a permanent sinus infection. He told Anders, "It's my job to tell you to use the tenth floor portas. It's your job to do with that info what you will. Long as I don't see or hear the alternatives I don't give a shit."

So, we set up our own bathroom, called it Latrine Row. Our crew wasn't the only crew to come up with this simple fix. But you stuck to your own latrine. Ours was on the twenty-first floor, which was where I was headed. A row of ten-gallon buckets in a penthouse suite, staged on the ledge of the upper floor deck, with a commanding view of the loft space and a panorama of lower Manhattan. You could piss in the bucket then shake your hind end or waggle your tip dry before saluting Battery Park or Wall Street. The Freedom Tower was out there, too, glass-clad and sleek, with Lady Liberty raising her torch in the distance. We kept fragrance gels in each bucket that kept the brine smelling sparkly-fresh as a soured case of gooseberry wine, and there was an eighty-pound bag of concrete mix with a scooper for the crap buckets. You'd be surprised how fast dry mix turns a turd to stone.

We kept Latrine Row under a blue tarp. Only a snoop might suspect something, peeling the tarp back to pry open a bucket lid. But the turds were always buried under concrete mix, and the piss buckets we could always claim as a finishing solvent. Not that there were any snoops. The entire work site being non-union, with a couple of high-paid union members there to feign a union presence, up to spec, up to code. No one was going to be looking at our crap buckets, or stirring a paint stick into our piss.

But there were a couple of show offs, Taser and Meathead Jack, who liked to skip Latrine Row to piss in the elevator shafts. Not me. Those shafts without passenger cars or doors dropped down into a deliriously long fall. I guess that was the thrill of pissing into the shaft, getting to watch the beads of your stream quivering into the void. But like I said, not me. There were too many pranksters on our crew who wouldn't hesitate to give you a false shove before yanking you back.

It was also where every crew from our floor up to the thirty-third floor dumped their latrine buckets at shift's end. It was always around 4:30pm when the piss started to shower down the shafts. Supposedly there were sump pumps there to pipe it street-level into a curbside drain. Just another check mark of illegal activities on the job. I'm sure Osmos knew about it too, but would probably never cop to it if hard-pressed on the matter. He seemed a site-manager, who was expert at not only staying out of sight, but most likely with the deft ability to dodge legalities should they ever come up. Let it all stick like poison darts to someone else, like Anders, or some other crew boss managing one of the many crews working this tower.

I pushed open the door to Latrine Row. They were both standing there pensively, Osmos and Anders. You could feel the heat from whatever had just been said still lingering between them. Osmos' thick and hairy hands were crossed behind his back, holding onto a collection of pink invoices. Then Anders signaled I should leave. On my way out, I closed the door by finger-hooking the hole where soon there would be a knob. So it seemed we were about to go another week without pay. I was glaring at three open elevator shafts, thinking it might be worth the vertigo, or maybe I'd just piss on the floor.

Then Taser appeared like a troubled sleepwalker. He was down the hall, shuffling toward me. There was a lost look in his eyes, the grubby lenses of his glasses set crooked on his nose. Maybe he'd heard the news of no pay too. A frantic radiance was still glimmering behind him, filling the doorway with a blue-white strobe from an arc welder's torch. Taser seemed to be working out a problem of his own, as if in his hands, mid-twist, was a broken Rubik's cube. Not once did he acknowledge me, as he ambled toward one of the open shafts, and whenever I rethink this moment I think how I should have shouted his name, or simply blocked him from that final step. Have you ever seen someone suddenly fall quietly from view?... You wonder, how could that be possible? That you never shouted his name, or attempted to keep it from happening. Best just to say, if anyone ever asks, there wasn't time to do anything. Only there was, and that's the clock you'll always see on the wall, the seconds you had with all the time in the world, and all you could do was just stand there and watch.

***

Hours later, I was on my way to Kyra's party, and it would be a party because we just got paid. Anders had checks for everyone at the end of the shift, not just for the week, back pay too. After an instant check-cashing place took its four percent cut, I was Friday night rich. Then it was, get me to the party, but first I needed a wad of food in my gut to sponge up the night of drinking ahead, so after the subway ride to Dutch Kills, I went to Big New York Chicken and Pizza for a couple of slices. News of the freaky heat wave was playing from the mini-flat screen bolted to the corner of the ceiling. The weather woman was talking about a swamp heat moving into the city like a smog monster of humidity. There were still a couple of holdout levees of dirty snow banked along the streets. But the heat was already moving in, my pores starting to ooze like the slice of cheese pizza drooping from my hand.

My other misread for the day had been thinking Taser had dropped twenty plus stories to his death, rather than just a couple of stories onto the roof of an elevator cab, one that had just been installed by God, though God didn't stop a clean-up crew from a few flights above from dumping their daily latrine bucket. I'd caught some of that rain too, a hefty splash across the back of my head and shoulders from where I'd wriggled up to the edge of the shaft to peer down into the hollow. There was Taser on top of the elevator, bent strangely, hair dripping wet with piss. His eyes shocked wide open. Then came the shouts booming down into the shaft to stop the elevator. He was still gasping as if someone had broken his back with a sledgehammer.

Then someone rapped against the window of the pizza parlor, and if the glass hadn't been there those knuckles would have been rapping against the back of my head. I turned and instantly noticed the scuzzy green eyebrows and back drape of hair. It was Nuclear Gene. In a stained undershirt and oversized army jacket, he stepped into the parlor and pulled the chair opposite me to sit facing another table. That was his style. If he ever looked your way it would be somewhere near your feet, or over your shoulder.

I bit into my slice and said, "Thought you'd be in Daytona by now."

He lurched with a reaching hand for the napkin dispenser.

"Daytona's going to have to wait."

He sat with a grunt then honked his nose, digging the napkin into his nostrils, as he told me how he'd miscalculated his winnings by a zero.

I said, "I thought you'd cashed out that card?"

He was still digging deep into his nose, widening one eye. "I did the following morning, realizing I'd just zeroed out my own cash buying all you fucks a night's worth of drinks. Bar booze adds up fast when you're pouring it into ten or more mouths. I woke up reamed and had to use the winnings to cover back rent. I'm still a month behind and all fucked broke, too, bro."

"Shit, man, that's rough."

I took a sip of ginger ale, a slow pull on the straw. Nuclear Gene glanced at the uneaten slice on my tray.

"Looks like somebody got paid, eating out on the town. I heard Anders got checks for everyone today. That's why I'm out here, figured he'd be at Kyra's party. I've got back pay coming, too, like three week's worth." He dropped the napkin to the floor, scooting it under the table with the toe of his sneaker as he reached into his jacket. He pulled out his burner phone, powered up the screen, then huffed, stuffing it back into his jacket. "I texted him an hour ago, still waiting to hear back." Then he looked toward the food counter at the tiered display of pizza pies, shelved behind a lengthy hot pane of glass.

"That pizza any good?"

"It's alright." I finished the first slice, leaving the crust on the paper plate. One more slice to go. "But I'm done. You want this other one?"

"Naw, man, I'm not looking for charity."

"You don't take it, I'm just going to throw it out."

"Well, that'd be a waste."

He grabbed the slice and was slow to chew the first bite as if assessing the overall flavor. Then he said he'd had better and with a shrug took another bite. I slurped up the final beads of ginger ale, the straw sounding off a hollow racket inside the can.

I said, "So, you been to Kyra's party?"

Gene had crammed over half the slice into his mouth and was working it down from the lump in his right cheek. "Yeah, that party sucks."

"What? Nobody there?"

"No, there's plenty of people there. It's just more of a vegan cracker, soft-sipping sort of bubbly-wine party.

Arty-poo small talk. MoMa Momma, PS1 hipster drivel, dipshits in tracksuits and boxy blazers. Got a couple of Wall Street cheese eaters there too. So, I'd say dress code's out for you, man. But you got an educated mind, you'll probably fit right in like a pig in gluten-free shit."

Then he finished up the slice, said he had a tab running at Slappy's, where next he was headed. Slappy's was a skank bar on the industrial outskirts of Greenpoint, red-lit rooms with people slithering in the dark. "A good place to fall into some ass," he said mid-chew on a wad of mozzarella. Whatever that means, the few times I'd been to Slappy's it smelled more like one big dirty ass than anything you'd want to fall into.

"Speaking of falls." Nuclear Gene flinched against his seat. "Goddamn heard about Taser. That dumb shit. Can't believe he didn't die. Hell was he doing? Heard he'd been staring into the arc light of the weld. Must have been smoked out of his mind. Blinding himself like that then moping around like Humpty Dumpty. You saw him take the fall?"

"Uh, yeah... like right when it was happening."

"Stupid shit's at the party, too, gimping around, still reeking damp of piss when he should be at the hospital getting that leg checked out. I heard you got splashed too. Whole bucket. Funny, I don't smell it on you."

"Well, come over here, give me a hug, you'll probably smell it on my jacket. I did give myself a water-hose shower to the head before leaving work."

"Man, that place is fucked." Gene fingered free a side-tooth gunk of cheese, swallowing it down. "Someone's going to die working there."

"Who's to say we're not all already dead in some way."

"Well put, poet."

His chair screeched and he stood and asked about the crust on my paper plate. I told him he could have that too. Then he folded it up and crammed it into his mouth. He never said goodbye, giving me a backhanded wave as he turned for the front door.

Under the red neon glow of the pizza sign in the window, I watched him ferret across the street, hands bunched in the pockets of his army jacket. Then I pondered the stains on my paper plate. Orange translucent spots. Like an oily divination. That whatever ass either of us would be falling into that night would probably be our own.

***

If the party had been arty-poo and rye crackers and stale conversation it had moved on, because now it was throbbing with industrial beats and a synth groove that rumbled in your bowels, but for the most part it was a non-dancing crowd, forty to fifty people dispersed in small chatty clusters. There were no overhead lights, a club atmosphere, color-filtered pin lights angled here and there, one pointing up at a tree-sized plant, throwing its shadows up the brick wall and turning its jungle-wide leaves deep sea blue. The warehouse windows overlooked an auto-body collision shop. Aside from the loft being one long open space, there was a row of rooms, and all the doors were closed, except for one with a bed that served as a dumping ground for coats, purses, and bags. I looked again at the closed doors, thinking Kyra had at least four other roommates aside from Stacy.

I continued to mill about the party, spotting a couple of coworkers, thankfully far enough away that I didn't feel obliged to step into their conversation. We simply acknowledged one other with a what-up tilt of the chin. I picked up the pace as if seeing someone I knew at the other end of the loft. I shouldered my way into a crowd of slobs in slacker pants and office workers undone at the collar. They were gathered around a card table, eager to place bets. Meathead Jack was sitting there with his hands tied behind his back. The only thing featured on the table was a candied head of ham. He said he could devour it whole in under fifteen minutes. I'd seen the act at other parties. No doubt about it, M.J. is a talented eater with Joey Chestnut powers of full-throated mastication. Kenyan John was massaging his shoulders, hyping him up for the big chow. Fonda was collecting bets, one being that M.J. wouldn't puke all over the place, Kyra threatening to beat his ass if he did. I surveyed the round of fired-up faces, not one of them being Stacy.

Then I saw someone that could be her, but my sightline was partially blocked by a couple who seemed ready to blow this party, disturbed by the meat-eating cheer. I was getting closer, certain now that it was her, yet still only able to see her from behind. She had on the same blue wig as the night we'd first met. In a shiny skinsuit, she was dancing with herself, the physique of her backside shimmering astronaut silver. Maybe this go-around we could talk sci-fi, Agnès Varda's *Les Créatures* or Chris Marker's *La Jetée*. Maybe I'd start things off with a sly quote from Tarkovsky's *Stalker*. That line about weakness being a great thing. I wondered if she'd catch it. I was drafting up a text on my phone as a glow-bright ruse to bump into her. But she turned around before I got to her. The sound system glitched into silence. I was face to face with a slender-hipped dude who appeared to be transitioning, eyes heavy on the mascara, face glittered silver, lips painted black.

I apologized for stepping too close. The music returned, now pulsing with a cavernous beat, astral synth, and gloomy vocals. The dancer swayed to the rhythm with a half-interested look that could have been an invitation, and not wanting to appear rude before turning away I shouted over the beats that I was looking for a bathroom. The dancer shrugged, continuing to sway to the beat.

Maybe Stacy was in one of these rooms. I started down the row of doors, the first one locked, the second one opening onto an empty room. The third one I shut as quickly as I had opened it, then stood there, thinking of whom I had just seen. It was Taser, seated at the end of a full-sized bed. I stepped back into the room, leaving the door open behind me.

The tension had eased somewhat from his face, though he still seemed somewhat caught off-guard and displeased to see me. When I'd first entered the room, he quickly hid something, and was sitting on it now, probably something he'd pilfered from the room, a hideaway stash of weed or prescription pills. Then there was the damp reek of all that piss that had splashed over him earlier in the day, still clinging to the husk of his work clothes, a piercing stink of ammonia, enough to water up my eyes.

He was still sitting there and I was still standing there. I think he was waiting for me to leave, his attention fixed somewhere between me and a Wham-O hula-hoop propped against the wall. What an odd man, with a round face and faint double chin sandpapered with stubble. The back of his head flat as a sheet pan, a physical trait of Polish men. One I hadn't inherited. I guess my distant bloodline was more Austrian and Spanish than Polish. Yet, I felt somehow related to him.

At work, he would make these strange... I won't say origami, but twisted figures out of leftover lunch napkins. It was enough to know that within him was a private world. At least he had that, the inclination to sculpt. I wondered if where he lived, one might find a world of these twisted little figures, on a bookshelf, or in the kitchen cabinets, or on a night stand.

I hadn't seen him since the accident, when a couple of the crew guys helped him off the elevator roof. He gimped away from their hold, insisting everything was fine. But I could tell the fall had knocked something out of him that still had yet to return, and seeing that made me feel partially to blame. I could have prevented it from happening.

"You alright?" I said.

He was squinting in my general direction, his grubby glasses still crooked on his nose. I continued to stand there, keeping the door open behind me. The sound of the party still between us, booming bass and the chatter of the crowd.

"I'm fine," he shouted. "I'll be right out."

"Okay, yeah." I turned to leave, then after a couple of steps stopped. What I really wanted to do was go back out into the party to find Stacy. You know, get into some conversation, but then the guilt returned and I don't know, I guess I wanted to make things right, or at least try, so I turned around and said, "You know some of us were talking, and uh, we were thinking maybe you should get things checked out."

"What?" he shouted.

"Hospital," I said.

"Yeah, yeah." He grimaced. "Everyone's been on my ass about it. I'm going. I'm going."

"Okay, well, maybe I-I could go with you. How about we call a car, or y-you feel like walking?"

"Walking? No," he said. "I feel like sitting. Look, really, I'm fine. I'd just rather be alone."

Shouts and cheers exploded from the party. M.J. must've gobbled into the head of ham past the midway mark. I thought to go and check it out but as I turned to leave I had a bad feeling, thinking of when I'd first entered the room, how Taser had been quick to hide something, something he was still sitting on, something I was thinking he now might try and use to hurt himself, or worse kill himself, so instead of leaving I closed the door behind me. He looked up at me annoyed.

"What are you doing, man? I told you I'm good."

"I figured I should just sit with you awhile."

"What you should do is fuck off. Look, I'm alright."

"Are you?"

Then I rushed up to him. It was quick, how he pelted me upside the head, three, four times. But I'd won the fight with his other hand, snatching out from under him what he'd been sitting on. My right ear was still ringing from having been struck. It wasn't a gun, or a bottle of pills, or even a razor, but a slinky pair of panties. I was staring at them in my hand, sleek and rosy red. They could have come from either the chest of drawers or the dirty hamper in the corner of the room.

"The fuck?!" His eyes were still bulging as if he'd been punched in the throat. "I told you to leave me alone."

I continued to stare at the panties slacked over my hand.

"You want 'em back?"

"No, I don't want 'em back. You fucking tainted 'em, man. Just go. Leave me alone."

I left the door wide open, and well, if I'd tainted his night he'd just pissed all over mine. I shoved my way through the crowd, got called a jerk, and stumbled over the welcome mat on my way out into the brightly lit hall. No one bothered shutting the door after me. Then it was a quick flight of stairs down. I banged out the metal front door and kept on walking.

***

The plan was to march back to my apartment, from Dutch Kills to Greenpoint to Bushwick. It'd be a hump getting there, several miles. I was done partying, but there was still the cock-eyed urge to get screaming drunk. I did have a pint of Captain Morgan's. I hate rum, too. I got it because I thought it would be a suave reveal at the party, pull that pirate from my pocket like an "Argh!" for anyone looking for a hearty sip. Sad, I know, an instance where the advertising worked. But, come on, who doesn't want to drink like a goddamn pirate?!

The humidity had finally squatted on the night and after marching several blocks I was drenched with sweat. My tee-shirt pasted across my back, I had my coat in the crook of my arm. Newton Creek, which was as wide as any river, smelled faintly septic with a Nutrasweet flavor of industrial solvents. I stopped midway over the Pulaski Bridge. There was a space designated for standing where you could look out onto the Manhattan skyline. This was just past the operator tower for the drawbridge. The control room was dark, but I'd heard somewhere that beneath the control room were several other rooms that served as living quarters. I wondered if there was a bridge operator living there now. I've often fantasized about living in such a tower, wondering what it would be like to have one room stacked on top of the other. It seemed a modest dream, one that could easily fit into the saying *anything is possible*. But I guess you'd have to know something about the mechanics to operate the bridge. It's probably straightforward until you open the operator's manual to a year's worth of technical specs. Ah, just keep spraying Krylon, bro. I slammed the entire pint of rum and it burned down my throat like turpentine with a butterscotch finish.

Soon as I was done dry retching I continued to stand there with both elbows planted on the rail. I'd tossed the bottle to stare at the panties in my hand, the silky rouge with a frilly waistline draped over my knuckles. Newton Creek's not a creek where the water flows, but a creek where the water stands unmoving, a scum green sheen topped with floaters of garbage. These could have been

Kyra's panties, or Stacy's, or one of their roomies. I'd never know, looking down at the dark green water.

Eventually I'd find out about Stacy. How she'd won a grant to Saint Petersburg, Russia to lead a workshop on modern dance. Then who knows what? Maybe she took the troupe on a global tour. I never heard more than that, or thought again about the name of Norma Desmond's chimp, except, well, maybe that it should be Chimp, because sometimes a chimp is just a chimp, right?

Then it was Monday morning, coffee, fist bumps, and "Hello Piss Boys" from the crew, with Fonda taking a whiff of me saying I still smelled like a urinal. It was Taser who'd gotten the biggest splash, but I was the one getting the biggest ribbing. I guess they all felt sorry for him. He was still limping around like a man blinded in one eye.

We ended up working together that day, sanding opposing ends of a balustrade rail to a smooth finish. By late afternoon we were chuckling over what we would call ourselves if we ever formed a grunge band. Certainly not Piss Boys. Two-Headed Dog was still a top contender. I think we both knew the band would never happen, but the friendship remained—enough so that he asked me one night, over beers at Slappy's: "Whatever happened to those panties?"

I told him about the Pulaski bridge, my standing there deep in contemplation, the drained pint of rum in one hand, the panties loosely clenched in the other, and the beautiful and lonesome whistling sound that pint made after I'd flicked it out onto the night air, watching it twirl before it struck into the distance with a soft splash. Then next came the panties. Those I let drop from my hands to watch them float on the water as if they might stay there forever before filling up wet, drowning darkly as a wilted rose.

"Damn." Taser anointed the loss with a tilt of the can before taking a somber sip. His face was bar-lit red, morose with shadows. Then his back smooched across the vinyl booth as he shouldered up to the wall with a private smile. Now we were both slacked against the wall, outside the cusp of light glowing on the table with a crimson hue. The silence stayed between us while the music thumped in the background. A song about bad company that sounded like good company, and it was good company being there with Taser, the two of us smiling, each of us in our own clutch of darkness.

Truth is, those panties are still in my room somewhere, if you asked where I wouldn't be able to tell you—but I can tell you how I kept on walking that night, through the moist and heady heat, keeping them in hand like a silky talisman. One that I'll always treasure.

MORE STARLIGHT, PLEASE

Two men. Orson Welles and Marlon Brando. They veered off-road somewhere in the Sonoran Desert. South of the border. They crashed into a saguaro cactus, over twenty feet high. The top swayed and dropped like an alien green chandelier. The roof of the car buckled. The windshield cracked. Steam hissed from under the engine hood. Orson's silver hair was askew as he stumbled out of the baby blue Coupe DeVille. A trickle of blood trailed from his eyebrow. He shouted out into the desert plain.

"Kiki!"

His toy poodle, black as the night. She was somewhere out there. She had bounded fast as a jackrabbit out the backseat window as soon as they had crashed into the saguaro. Again, he shouted her name, his voice booming out among the cacti and desert scrub.

Brando was outside the Coupe DeVille sizing up the damage. The saguaro, pronged with a hefty multitude of spiny arms, would take at least five men with push brooms to prod off the car. Then Brando gawked up at the starry night sky and swept both of his hands over his thick white hair as he continued to gaze up into the cosmos, the Milky Way a phantasmagoric spunk on all of outer space. He remained in awe.

"Kiki!"

Welles' shouts were waning. Still he was hoping to see the phosphorous orbs of her eyes, somewhere out there blinking back at him, but all he could see was what surrounded him—more scrub weed, ocotillo, and those imposingly tall cacti. Some thirty, forty feet high. Were they crowding in on him? That was the feeling prickling under his skin like millipedes. The desert seemed to be breathing, the cacti stepping closer, then shuddering away. Was he losing his mind? He'd felt funny even before the accident, feeling the skin wanting to melt from his face. But he was still there, corpulent and stentorian, in his beige trench coat, trousers, and waxed shoes. He shouted again.

"Kiki!"

The wind whistled across the desert plain. He didn't want her out there, not with the creatures of the night, patient predators, cold-blooded, hot-blooded, serpent's tongue, incisors, fangs, tusks. Again, he shouted her name. To nothing but the wind and the darkness beyond.

This nightmare collision with the gargantuan cactus had been Brando's fault. Brando. That cream-faced loon. What was he doing? Orson turned to see. The pompous ape. He was standing there with cock in hand urinating on the Coupe DeVille.

"Some run in, hey?" Brando was smirking as he guided the arc line of his piss across the rear fender. A golden splatter.

That was it.

Welles charged into him. The two men scuffled,

blubbery as sumo wrestlers. Brando in Mexican sandals was struggling to keep a foothold. Welles with two pudgy fistfuls had him by the Acapulco shirt. Piss freckled across the thighs of Welles' trousers. Then with a subtle leap the two men swerved off balance. The ground coughed from the combined weight of their fall.

Orson floundered for top position, smearing Brando's fat face half flat with the heel of his hand. Brando was coughing with laughter, pushing at Welles with one arm. Welles shoved harder, a noxious gleam hatching in his eyes. Was this what he had wanted all along? To bash in Brando's head. There was a desert rock, jagged enough, large enough, to do the job.

Brando saw it too. Welles scrambled to pick it up. Brando grinning up at him.

"Do it, brother. Do it."

***

Earlier the only violence between them had been nothing more than the sounds of dull steak knives struggling to cut through tough meat. This was at a flat-roof shack miles from La Zorra, Gotas de Oro. Brando's pick. He had pointed at it from the Coupe DeVille.

"We eat there."

Welles cringed when they pulled up to the place, fearing that entry alone would blow out his bowels. But he was following Brando's lead, and soon wanting Brando to follow his. For it was Welles who had driven from Hollywood Hills to La Zorra to pitch Brando on a bit-part in his film adaptation of *The Merchant of Venice*.

The cook with tarred teeth and cow's blood spattered on his chef's coat was also their waiter. They were the only ones there, except for Kiki on Welles' lap, her wet eyes blinking, patiently waiting for their food to arrive.

Brando smacked his neck, then looked at his hand and around the restaurant for the mosquito. Decorative fly strips hung over every table, each strip tacked with red-and-pink rose petals, an inventive flourish Welles had privately noted to himself, as quaint as rosebuds on a steaming heap of garbage.

At Brando's insistence, their order was the same. Dinner was served on clay plates. Hanger steak with chunky cactus sauce, fried plantains, and port wine. Orson bared his teeth as he strained to swallow another gulp. It was time to lure Brando into the role. He placed the tin cup on the table.

"You'll play Old Gobbo. The blind father of Lancelot. Don't worry." Welles tapped his hand near Brando's plate. "I'll feed you your lines."

Brando was chewing with his mouth open. "How you like the steak?"

"This?" Welles looked at the food on his clay plate. "I'd say this is only the finest in queasy cuisine. In fact, I'm surprised it didn't come served on a hubcap." Then he leaned forward, lowered his voice. "You think the chef's actually an auto mechanic in disguise?"

"You're good," Brando said, forking up another bite, talking mid-chew. "I don't like suck-ups. I thought you might be the biggest suck-up of all. But your tongue says lousy. You say lousy. That's good."

"Wine's palatable." Welles took another painful sip. "But only enough for washing this boiled grub down."

Then Brando's face dropped. There was a lost look in his eyes, as if wherever he looked nothing was there. No Orson. No Kiki. No Gotas de Oro.

"Like this?" he said. "You want me to play Old Gobbo like this?"

He placed his silverware on the table and started to blindly touch his food. Welles winced at the act, but was mildly amused, seeing potential in it. Then Brando reclaimed his vision, licking the palms of his hands and fingertips clean, with a zesty relish flaring across his eyes.

Kiki yipped for a bite of her food, which Welles produced from a side dish. Her food was the same as theirs, but to his surprise she didn't want it. Gritting her teeth, she turned her head as he offered her a forkful of steak with cactus sauce. It was rare for Kiki to recoil from eating meat, just as it was for Welles. But this hanger steak was lousy enough to kill a man. Especially that cactus sauce.

"So, I'll consider the part." Brando signaled with his chin. "But you better be a good *muchacho*. Eat all that up. And I mean all of it. See, much as I like the fact you're not a suck-up with your opinion, you're going to suck all that up, because that's my *jefe* in there, and he don't like to see food come back into the kitchen."

Welles studied his plate.

"So, I eat this, you play Old Gobbo? We haven't even discussed fees."

"That's my fee." Brando angled the tines of his fork at Welles' plate. Then the food suddenly seemed delectable to Orson. Except for the cactus sauce, which he scraped to the side.

"No, you eat it all!"

With a thwack of the fork, Brando cracked the rim of Welles' plate. Kiki growled.

"That means the cactus sauce too." Brando grinned.

"What is it?"

Welles' lips shriveled at the thought of eating the chunky aloe sauce.

"A gateway to the stars." Brando smiled, triumphant.

Welles jerked back in his seat.

"What, are you trying to poison me?"

Then Brando clawed up a slimy bite of Welles' cactus sauce, slurped it up with a pleased grin.

"Now eat up and to the stars we'll go, with me as Old Gobbo."

"The stars," Welles said with a cocked eyebrow. "You say that like a slick-haired loaf in a lawn chair eager to sell Hollywood maps... to the stars."

"And you say that... " Brando fattened his cheeks chubby with cactus sauce, "like one of those stars that's no longer on the map."

"Oh, but a dagger to the liver you plant," Welles said. "Well put, but last I checked I'm still on the map."

"Look, you want this?" Brando struck himself blind again. "Then go on. Take a bite. Tell Old Gobbo what to say?"

The first thing Welles swallowed was a dab of air. Kiki was whimpering on his lap. Then Welles cut into the rank meat, swabbing a bite into the cactus sauce.

"By God sonties, 'twill be a hard way to hit." Welles opened his mouth.

Brando repeated the line, then said, "What's son-ties?" Welles started cutting into another bite.

"An exclamation of surprise."

"Well, then, get ready," Brando said. "Because soon as you finish that up 'By God sonties' is where we're headed next."

***

After dinner, they drove out into the desert—Route 2, miles of open road, it seemed they could drive for hours and still be headed nowhere. That's when Welles started to feel the millipedes crawling under the skin of his arms and neck, and the phrase "By God sonties" jumped out of his skull. The air between him and the windshield and everything outside was suddenly alive, hypnotic as the cellular activity you'd see under a microscope, only with an ectoplasmic sheen, a shimmering incandescence, swimming all around him. His grip floated up and off the steering wheel like a couple of meaty hand balloons. And all of this in a single breath. Then Brando jammed his foot on top of Orson's foot, slamming the gas pedal.

They veered off-road.

A chuff of desert dust cleared from the windshield. They were rumbling out onto the desert plain. Kiki was floating midair as she bounced around the backseat bench. The head beams jittered out into the night. The red needle on the speedometer climbed—50, 60, 70.

Brando kept Welles' foot and the gas pedal mashed under his. Welles was thrashing at Brando, who now had one hand gripped on the steering wheel. Brando, maniacal with glee, was grinning back at Welles until SLAM!

The saguaro cactus, a cold shadow in the night, with a half dozen arms, snapped mid-waist, over a thousand pounds. The rooftop crunched under the weight of its fall and Kiki bolted from the Coupe DeVille. There then gone—just a spit of sand from where she had vanished in the night. Welles stumbled from the car. The engine hissed under the buckled hood. A wisp of steam stirred across his face as he shouted out into the desert.

"Kiki!"

Then Brando was pissing on his car. Welles knocked him to the ground and soon Brando was looking up at the rock in Welles' hand.

Brando said, "Do it, brother. Do it."

But Welles shuddered, losing his grip. The rock dropped from his hold. He slumped forward, planting his hands on the ground above Brando's shoulders. It seemed Welles was on the verge of laughter, with his mouth wide open.

There was expectancy in Brando's eyes, his pupils fully dilated, a shivering schism in their depths, accepting what was to come with a knowing smile.

Welles threw up. Brando shielded himself against the hot splatter flushing from Welles' mouth. When Welles was done he flopped onto his backside. But he wasn't done. He rolled on to his side to retch some more.

"That's to be expected," Brando said, sitting upright. He shook the vomit from his hands, wiped the sludge from his face with his Acapulco shirt.

Now Welles was flattened on his back with an unplugged look in his eyes. His voice was raspy.

"You did poison me, didn't you?"

"You mean *us*," Brando said. "Poisoned *us*."

Then he turned away from Welles to throw up in the sand. But there was no consolation in Brando's puking. It was more for Welles an echoing of the violence that had spewed from his own mouth. A film loop reeled in his mind's eye. An apple in outer space on a carpet ride of vomit. There was Brando as Adam and Welles as Adam. Two mouths as nebulae competing for the apple. Welles couldn't make it go away, no matter how hard he shut his eyes, the starlight was still there. Their heads were roasted and glazed, face to face on a silver platter, the apple pulsing arrhythmically between their lips.

"I don't want to die." Orson gasped.

"Then don't." Brando snuggled up to him like a bedmate and placed his hand on Welles' breast.

"Just breathe. Relax. Don't try to fight it. Or it will rear its ugly head."

"What's happening to me?"

"Peyote-ote-ote," Brando said. "This should take us back about twenty thousand years."

"Peyote?" Welles turned on his side and crammed a finger into his mouth to retch up the poison.

"That'll only heighten the ride," Brando said. Then Welles settled again on his back, staring up at the sky. "Why did you give me peyote?"

"*Us*," Brando said. "*Us*."

Peyote. Mushrooms. LSD. Welles had been to parties. Hollywood Hills. France. Italy. He'd seen the eyes of those hallucinating. Movie producers. Actors. Actresses. Oil men. Sheik philosophers. All of them babbling like mystic boobs. Like Brando now, with vomit on his chin. Welles had steered clear. He'd wanted nothing to do with tearing into the fabric of the cosmos. Such a peek-aboo seemed a gamble with insanity. Brando his case-in-point, who was now rambling about hagfish and how they didn't have eyes.

"But rather light-sensing organs." Brando was on his back with his hands folded across his chest. "What I'm talking about is the origin of the eye. It started with light-sensing organs that looked like worms." Brando's hands started to come to life as if in conversation with each other. "See, I think this should be part of Old Gobbo's part. Now if he can't see then that's part of his plight, no? What if he's working on a braille manifesto about what it means to see? No, no, wait. Wait. What if he's a craftsman, a maker of glass eyes? Now that! That's the true Merchant of Venice."

Welles decided to let Brando ramble, knowing there'd be no use in explaining anything more to him about Old Gobbo. Maybe this was Welles' part, the one he'd come to La Zorra to play. He had pulled off the road on his way there, to film himself as Shylock from *The Merchant of Venice*, in his beige trench coat with a burgundy sky as his desert backdrop.

Shylock had said, "I will buy with you, sell with you, talk with you, walk with you and so following, but I will not eat with you, drink with you, nor pray with you."

But Welles had eaten with Brando, had drunk with Brando, and now was in a desperate state having to pray with Brando. Welles was losing touch with why he'd driven to La Zorra. Was it to be somewhere where nobody saw you for your name? There were shadows upon shadows looming there in the desert, Brando seemingly content with their shifty presence.

Then there was Kiki.

Oh, sweet Kiki.

Welles opened his arms. She was charging toward them.

She bounded up onto Welles' chest only to leap off his shoulder. Both Brando and Welles looked back to where she vanished once again into the desert. Then they turned to look at what she'd been running from.

What was coming toward them from out of the dark? Was it a herd, or a beast alone? By way of peyote, it sounded like the hungry cry of a thousand heads on four legs, or was it a single head on a thousand legs?

Whatever it was, it would soon be upon them. They maintained their position, eyes wide, elbows propped on the sand, as if staring from a beach out to sea. The opacity of Brando appeared more and more to dim, yet he was always there, a cunning smile. Welles didn't even have to look anymore, blindly staring like Old Gobbo. Now he could hear the rumbling of hooves upon the earth as it must have been twenty thousand years ago.

Just breathe it in.

HAND FOR THREE

He wouldn't know his own name if you asked him. His ears were still ringing from the explosion. He'd been slammed to the ground and was staggering upright. Everything was jarringly unfamiliar—the time of night, the surrounding woods, why he'd been running and from whom. There was dirt in his hair, dirt on his teeth. His face was coal black with soot. He started running. He had on only one shoe, his other foot in just a sock. He dropped to the ground. Something had stabbed into the sole of his foot. The pain shot straight to his mouth. A flashlight appeared in the distance. The beam of light was steadily approaching through darkened trees. He kept his hands clamped over his mouth.

He soon realized it wasn't a flashlight getting closer, but a headlamp. Only once did it shine near him. Minutes after the light's retreat, he struggled to stand, leaning against a tree for support. Even in the dark he could see his sock was soaked with blood. His leg was starting to feel numb from all the pain. A chill rushed through him. The sky, an apocalyptic gray, clung to the treetops.

He began to limp at a meditative pace, heel, foot...

breath in... heel, foot... breath out. Eyes anxiously wide, he scanned the forest, waiting for the headlamp to reappear. He searched the ground. The surrounding deadwood was too cumbersome or brittle to use as a weapon. He picked up a sizeable rock, then saw the light again. It was shining, deep in the distance, no longer roaming, but angled low to the ground, focused. He tightened his grip on the rock. He figured if he maintained his methodical pace he could get there without being detected.

***

The watcher was quietly stationed behind a nearby tree. The man with the headlamp was walking with a skillet in his only hand. A wadded t-shirt for a bandage had been duct-taped to the shoulder of his missing arm. Naked in a pair of grubby panties and cowboy boots, he crouched before a portable stove. Behind him was a camper van parked on four flat tires in front of the rear wall of a small and windowless concrete building. The watcher figured there must be some sort of back road leading out of this place.

Skillet continued to prime the fuel canister, a squeaky hiss every time he pumped. With his only hand, he struck the stove ablaze. The glow from the flame shimmered against the bone lines of his shins. Whatever was cooking on the stove, he was gnawing on his upper lip like it wasn't heating up fast enough. That's when he spoke from the side of his mouth to the watcher behind the tree.

"Back so soon?"

The slithery tone of his voice was familiar. The watcher limped out into the open, leaving the rock behind. Skillet snorted up a wad of black mucus and spat it on the ground. The watcher, gimping across the open lot, still felt like a stranger in this somehow familiar land.

"What's with your foot?" Skillet said.

The watcher, saying nothing, glanced at the camper van. The sliding door was open. There was someone lying there, suspended in a mesh-weave hammock. The watcher sat on a beer cooler with a backside view of Skillet still crouched before the stove. Whatever was hissing on the pan had the faint stink of burnt hair. That too was familiar. The watcher was disturbed by the grumbling in his gut hankering for a bite. He lifted the ankle of his injured foot, setting it on the knee of his other leg. Blood was dripping from the sole of his sock.

"How close you get this time?" Skillet said. "Must've been close enough to get tossed like a rag doll through the woods. 'Cause that's how you look. Truth is, I don't know why you thought it'd be any different. Only a fool would go out there. We heard the blast, too, figured you'd be in about five pieces."

Blood continued to drip from the heel of his sock. Skillet dinged the pan and with apprehension looked out into the woods. Then he looked back at the watcher, his headlamp shining brightly.

"Damn! Something got your foot good. You get cut?"

The watcher was squinting against the glare of the headlamp, about to reply, when Skillet shouted at the van.

"Carl! Get Jenkins a shirt or something to bandage his foot."

"*You* get it!" shouted a voice from the van.

"I can't get it. I'm cooking, 'member?!... *god*."

Skillet shook his head. The watcher realized that his name must be Jenkins and he mouthed the name silently, hoping it might feel familiar, but it didn't. Then he looked toward the van. The man, lumbering out into the open, had bonked his head and was rubbing it, as he slowed to a standstill.

"I was napping. Napping good too. Why you fuck me out of my nap?!"

"Sure, you were," Skillet said. "I bet it was a *nice* nap too."

Then Skillet winked at Jenkins with a masturbatory waggle of the hand. But Jenkins was still hoping for a cog of recognition to click into place over the man who'd appeared from the van. He was a big man, too, more flab than muscle, in a shredded dress shirt, one size too small, his gray pants in tatters at the knees, a pair of penny loafers stretched over his feet, a big toe budding from a hole in his left shoe.

The most disturbing thing about Carl was that he didn't have any eyes. Where they should've been it seemed the skin had melted over the sockets, as if at some point he'd tried washing his face with a handful of hot coals. Carl continued to meander among the contractor bags, plopped about the backlot, dozens of them, knotted up, fat and full as prehistoric eggs. He leaned over one of the tubby bags, blindly fumbling with the knot.

Skillet noticed how unfamiliar everything seemed to Jenkins.

"You alright?" he said. "You look more shook up than usual."

"Yeah, yeah, fine," Jenkins said, after peeling the bloodied sock from his foot, but it was a lie. He had no idea what was going on, or how he'd come to know these two men. It was all so disturbing—Skillet's missing arm and Carl's burned out eyes. Jenkins hoped that a memory or two would soon appear from the black fog in his mind.

He looked at the woods with the uncanny feeling of being watched. The fact that Skillet and Carl seemed relaxed, or resigned to whatever might be out there, helped to alleviate Jenkin's paranoia. Then he winced at the gash on the sole of his foot. The blood had congealed into a tender gleam.

Carl rustled inside a contractor bag, then gave up with a scowl. He held the sagging bag upright with a double-fisted grip and shook it, sneering in Skillet's general direction.

"You been moving these bags on me?!"

Skillet snapped, "That's not the bag with shirts, *fool*. That's the bag full of explosives. You know, like the bag you flicked a lighter to look inside one night. The one that blew your face out. Only that bag's got enough to blow us all to kingdom come. So, stop fooling with it, shaking it like you want to blow us all up. Now the bag you want with shirts is over to the right. Like I originally told you."

Carl grumbled as if wanting to strangle Skillet, "told you, hold you by the neck." He knotted the bag with an angry shove of the hands.

"What did I say?" Skillet hammered a fist against the air. "Go easy with that bag, *fool!*"

Carl thumped his own chest like a gorilla.

"You shouldn't have woken me up from my nap!"

Then Jenkins stood on his one good leg, ready to limp. "Show me the bag. I-I can get it."

"No, let Carl get it. He ain't done nothing but napping all day."

"Yeah, let me get it." Carl said, giving Skillet the middle finger. "I've been napping all day." He started searching for the next bag, feeling for it with his penny loafers while he kept his middle finger up for everyone to see.

"You know it's a good thing we ain't shooting at each other," Skillet said. "'Cause where you're aiming that finger you'd have just blown Jenkins' head clear off his shoulders."

Then Skillet smiled at Jenkins who gave him a weak smile in return. Whatever was frying on the stove was starting to stink like scorched meat. Jenkins said, "I-I think whatever's cooking's burning."

"No, no, no, not that one!" Skillet stepped up from the stove. "God, the rate you're going, Jenkins'll bleed out his foot, be dead by morning." Carl was still fumbling with another bag. Skillet marched toward him, raising his arm as if to throttle him single-handed. "What is it with you? Going left when I told you to go right."

"Well, I am blind! You ignoramus!"

They continued shouting at each other, Skillet shoving Carl toward another bag, Carl telling him to quit, that if he wasn't blind he'd beat his ass down. The moment might have amused Jenkins had he not finally seen what was cooking on the stove. He limped up to it, only to gawk in absolute horror. He knew something meaty had been burning on the stove. But what *kind* of meat he could have never fathomed. A human hand! Charred black with fingernails translucent as shrimp shells waiting to be peeled. Jenkins reeled back, flailing as he tripped over his own feet.

Where he fell, the cooler flipped open. His eyes widened over the gory sight. Wedged inside the cooler, cleaved of its hand and bent at the elbow, was what must've been Skillet's amputated arm. Jenkins scrambled upright, hobbling into a crippled sprint, coughing and choking, as he rushed to get to the other side of the building. At least from there he would be able to collect his thoughts. But as he reached the other side, he was stunned to see the same van and the same hand cooking on the stove.

Skillet was still shouting at Carl: "This! This is the bag of shirts!"

Carl was shouting back: "That's not where I left the bag of shirts. You moved it!"

Jenkins continued to rush back and forth along the side of the building, astounded each time he peered around the corner, the same back lot at both ends of the building, Skillet and Carl still in a shouting match, until finally Jenkins stepped into the lot and Skillet greeted him with a triumphant grin, shirt raised in hand.

"Looky here, my man! We finally got you a tee shirt to bandage up your foot."

But Jenkins was breathing too heavily to accept the shirt, leaning with his hands on his knees. Skillet was still dangling the shirt before him with a grin.

"Looks like you worked up a sweat. You know you shouldn't be running like that. Give your foot some time to heal. Otherwise ... " Skillet draped the shirt over Jenkins' shoulder like a gym towel. "Could end up losing that foot to an infection. Then no one could eat it." Skillet tittered to himself. "And that wouldn't be fair, considering." He gestured with his only hand toward his other hand still burning on the pan.

"What is this place?" Jenkins said, mopping the sweat from his face. He looked at the building before opening the shirt wide. A craze of dread filled his eyes. The shirt was spotted with blood. Then there was Skillet grinning back at him like, "Whadya mean, what is this place?" As if Jenkins should know. But he didn't. He was still looking at the shirt in his hands.

"Whose blood is this?"

"How should I know," Skillet said. "It's not like we been keeping tabs on whose bloody shirt is whose." Then Skillet leaned toward Jenkins with concern. "You sure you're okay?"

But it was too much—the blood on the shirt, the burnt hand on the pan, the building that kept leading you back to the same place, no matter how much you rushed around it. The whites of Jenkin's eyes fluttered into full view as he collapsed on the ground.

"What happened?" Carl said.

Skillet shrugged. "Tuckered himself out. Fainted"

He looked toward the woods, then back at the hand on the stove, and then back at Carl. "Guess that means more for me and you, buddy."

"What, we going to cut him up?"

"No, idiot. He ain't dead. But I ain't waiting for him to come to, neither. That there hand's good and ready."

"Well, we could save him a cut."

"You save him a cut. Me? I'm eating my half and I get the thumb too. Don't pout about it, neither."

"Well, it is your hand."

Then Carl looked to the ground as if near his feet was where Jenkins had collapsed, though Jenkins was several feet behind him, far to the right.

"Sorry friend, looks like you picked a bad time to pass out."

"Bad time for him." Skillet sucker-punched Carl's upper arm. "Good time for us!"

Carl hunkered into a defensive pose, waiting for the next strike.

"Good eats too," Skillet said, "if you can get to it before me." He pushed Carl and Carl grabbed him by the wrists, forcing him to the ground. Skillet kicked back and Carl stumbled toward the stove.

Skillet shouted, "Slow up you fucking idiot, you'll run right over dinner."

As if saying that could've kept it from happening. Carl tripped over the stove and it flipped onto a bag. Gas spilled everywhere. Skillet scrambled over to a trail of flames, throwing dirt on it and spanking it out with his hand, relieved it hadn't reached the bag of dynamite. But then he looked at where the stove had landed and realized his mistake, as the flames ate through the bag. The blast seared into view with a ground-shaking boom.

After the smoke cleared there were two dead men—one brained by shrapnel, the other disemboweled by the blast. Jenkins coughed himself awake. Small fires burned all around him. He struggled to sit half-upright. Then he saw the bodies. With a pained expression, he curled onto his side. The pan-fried hand was facing him. He thought of Skillet and Carl and remembered Skillet's true name. He stared a long time into the flames of one of the small fires, then looked again at the two dead men.

He said their names.

STILL LIFE OF A USED DESSERT FORK

She never said her name. He thought it was a prank call. Then she started talking about a photograph he'd taken over fifteen years ago. He didn't know how she could have acquired a framed print of his work. He thought he had destroyed them all. She wanted the photograph as wall art for a thrift store she was opening in West Asheville, North Carolina. She wouldn't tell him what was in the photograph, but the breathiness of her enthusiasm never stopped tingling in his ear.

"It's trashy. It's daring. And I love it. Love. It. I want everyone who comes to my store to see it! It speaks of a time, the spirit, the essence of what my store is going to be all about. Now I can't *pay* you for it. But I *promish* you a spotlight on the wall. What do you say?"

She sounded drunk. He wondered if she'd even remember making this call. It was after midnight. He kicked off his work shoes, loosened his cater-waiter bow tie and sat with a sigh as he unbuttoned his collar.

"And how did you get my number?"

After Midnight told him she got it the same way she

had acquired the photograph: from an old friend of his, Ross.

It was true he'd left a bunch of crap at Ross's parents' house before moving to Queens, New York sixteen years ago. He figured whatever he'd left in their attic must've turned to black mold, but maybe not. He wondered if they were still living in that two-story house with the rust-stained roof, off that winding gravel road in Candler. He always liked going there, the long strong hugs Ross's parents would give him, the house tainted with the sweet musty odor of stale sweat. They were hoarders, boxes and varied junk piles everywhere. He wondered how After Midnight could have burrowed her way into their attic. She did say she was opening a thrift store. Maybe Ross's parents had died, leaving behind a legacy of knick-knacks and clothes. Jim had hugged those too, nights he and Ross got cross-eyed drunk on Everclear. He'd always find a nice mound to pass out on, a slovenly hump of silky lingerie and high-heeled shoes. He owed Ross a call. About seven years overdue.

"Hello?" After Midnight said.

"Yeah, I'm thinking about it."

Jim was bopping an empty two-liter bottle of Mountain Dew against his knee, surveying his studio apartment, a neatly made bed, a thriving fern, a heap of clothes on an overstuffed hamper.

"How do you know it's mine?"

"Oh, it's yours, honey." She chuckled. "Unless someone else forged your signature on it."

A blush rose up the side of his neck. What had he been thinking all those years signing his photographs like a landscape painter? He squeezed the empty two-liter bottle. It crinkled in on itself.

"I think it's cute." She tittered with a smoker's rasp. "Adds authenticity to the picture."

"I don't know." He flipped the two-liter bottle like a frustrated juggler. It popped onto the carpeted floor, regaining its original form. "How about sending me a picture of the photograph with your phone. I'd like to see it before giving it the A-ok."

"But that'd ruin the surprise," she said. "Look, why don't you come to the opening of the store, and if you don't like it..." She gulped from whatever she was drinking. "I can take it down." He could hear her setting her glass onto a hard surface. She said, "You know, there's other *pishers* I can put up in its place. But really, don't overthink this. Just say, 'Yes,' then come down here and say, 'No,' if that's what you want."

Truth was, he didn't want to go back to Asheville and if he did, he didn't want to see any of his old work, knowing how disappointed he'd feel. He'd *had* his years in New York as a photographer. The pinnacle of his career was an unsold photograph in a group show at a gallery that had turned into a CVS drug store over eight years ago.

The photograph was of a used dessert fork. He was collecting them at the time and had dozens of them, some stand-alone, others wrapped in cloth napkins. His then-roommate asked to borrow a pen one night and after opening several of Jim's desk drawers, all of them loaded with dirty forks, he insisted, more seriously than half-jokingly, that Jim check himself into a psych ward—and that was without Jim letting him know every fork had a name.

All of them were named after women he had served and admired from afar—a fact he kept to himself and nothing you'd find anywhere near his artist statement. Rarely did any of the women have name tags so he'd make them up, prefacing it with whatever dessert they'd had. There was Cupcake Donna, Red Velvet Miyoshi, Cream Tart Adamma...

He decided to keep the collection, ditch the roommate, and find a place to live on his own. It was a year later, after working a party-boat ride on the East River, that he returned to his studio apartment disgusted with himself. He slammed the front door as quickly as he had opened it, still feeling he was on the boat, teetering about the apartment. His therapist was right, these used dessert forks as cherished photography subjects were stand-ins for an impotent form of the courtship ritual. He couldn't take it any longer, throwing away the Créme Brûlée Susie fork instead of staging her freshly creamed tines under the studio lights around his bed.

This was after another series of rejections, this round from coffee shops in West Orange, New Jersey. He had already spent most of the year canvassing other coffee shops in Queens, Brooklyn, Manhattan, and Staten Island. He'd even approached a funeral parlor, with the portrait of a polished dessert fork on a stately windowsill, a blood-orange sunset softly out of focus in the background. He used to take pictures on the sly, street photography, candid moments of strangers in motion. Then he got hooked on the forks.

It was time to bag it all up. He packed his whole collection, along with the photography equipment, into contractor bags for curbside pick-up. The following morning his coffee was more bitter than usual. He sipped as he watched two garbage men, up on the street, hoist the bags into the compactor truck. That had been seven years ago.

"You still there?" After Midnight said.

He kicked the empty two-liter bottle. It rolled up to the foot of his bed. What was it he'd said to Ross after leaving that boxful of framed prints in the attic? "Someday these pictures'll be worth more than your Dodge truck." He continued to stare at the floor, a weariness glassing over his eyes.

"Hello-o-o-o?"

And now fast forward to the middle of your forties and this half-drunk lady wants to put one of your pictures on the wall of her thrift store. Can't *pay* you anything for it. But people will see it while rooting around fussy bins of clothes for a bargain find. That's something, right?

"Okay." She sighed. "I'm hanging up."

In a fit, he started scrubbing the phone against the thigh of his polyester tux pants. She must have heard it as a signal problem.

"Can you hear me? I-I think we have a bad connection."

He raised the phone, talked at it from arm's length.

"I'm sorry, my phone does this sometimes—"

He ended the call, powered the phone down, flung it to the heap of clothes on the hamper. Then he moaned into the meat of his palms and when he was done slacked back against the sofa as if he'd just been drained of several pints of blood. The nails were still in the walls where his photographs had once hung. If he'd had the energy to stand, he would have flicked off the lights instead of staying on the sofa with a pillow over his head.

***

Breakfast was a bowl of autumn wheat with craisins. He'd slept past noon. There was still a dribble of milk on his chin which he wiped away with the back of his hand. He twisted the rod to the Venetian blinds. A basement window with a street-level view. The tawny slats revealed an overcast day far above the hubcaps of several parked cars. He could hear two boys playfully chasing each other. He dug into the hamper pile of dirty clothes. Retrieving his phone, he powered it back up. The Nokia screen glowed aquatic blue. Thirteen missed calls. He shook his head. "Crazy lady."

The outside pitter-patter of sneakers faded with one last clap of laughter. Maybe he would go to Asheville. It would be good to see Ross again. Cruise the old haunts—Chicken Hill and the French Broad River industrial district, both of which had had big makeovers, once ratty and desolate, now gentrified with artist's studios, fine dining, and riverside parks. A grin lurched up the side of Jim's face. There were microbreweries to be toured, the Blue Ridge Parkway, those craggy mountains, and starlight galore. And don't forget that sweet mountain smell, black soil moist as chocolate cake, almost good enough to eat.

He stumbled into last night's tux pants. This was after he re-tightened his lumbar corset, sucking in his gut to maximize the Velcro's hold. He suited up in his dress shirt, leaving it two buttons shy of the collar. Then with sink water and a paper towel, he shined his shoes.

The 7 train was standing room only. The subway shuttled along an elevated track. An expansive view of Queens, building rooftops and construction sites, distant high-rise cranes, the train slowly making its way to Manhattan. The passengers, seated and standing, were either gazing at their phones or toward some middle distance as if sleeping with their eyes wide open. But Jim was standing there, still thinking about Asheville with a lingering glee.

"To go or not to go," he mumbled as the train screeched a hard right. He wondered just how pretentious a crowd might be at a thrift-store opening. He would purchase two plastic swords from F.A.O. Schwartz and, once in Asheville, snip the protective beading from the tips. Ross would know the deal. They used to thrive on antics like that. Show up to wine-and-cheese parties with plastic swords and spearhead the tips with cheese cubes. See how far one could flick a cube for the other to catch with his mouth. But it never happened; the cubes of gouda and cheddar always bounced off someone else's head.

And so what if you run into old friends who have grown up to raise their own families, already in the third or fourth quarter of a career, warming up to the beach waters of early retirement, the traveling they'll do from the manna growing like fungus off a 401(k). Let them eat cheese too. Jim would talk about his great city conquests—the seared duck he'd served to diplomats, and the bacon-wrapped scallop P. Diddy thanked him for, saying, "Keep the toothpick."

Yeah, that's how he'll swashbuckle his way through the small talk, flick some cheese, maybe even spin a silver tray on his fingertip. Sure, this was speculation hinged with bitter irony on a platter full of angst that could easily topple onto someone's lap, but he had already bought into the What-Me-Worry farce of a Mad-Magazine trip—what it would be like to return to Asheville. It was a feeling he trusted. The dead weight from succumbing to a routine life was beginning to lift from his back, shucking from his spine those pesky barnacles of lost time.

Yes! It was imperative to see Ross again. Blind each other with pure grain alcohol. He could already hear that emptied bottle of Everclear twirling out into the night like an exclamation point waiting to silently explode, Ross and Jim shouting like gods from the commanding view of an off-road ledge, miles above a distant sparkle of city lights, only to hear their own voices shouting back... *It's been too damn long.*

He almost missed his stop. The 7 train door clipped his heel. On the platform he smooched an elderly woman on the forehead. She clutched her purse, glared at him savagely. He sprinted for the exit, spry and dapper as a gent about to leap and click his heels.

He knew he was revving himself up, but thirteen missed calls? After Midnight must really want him there. He would have to ask Ross about her too. He had yet to check the messages. Could be thirteen missed butt dials, or that she and Ross are tight as a pretzel. But who cares? He was going to Asheville. He'd call Ross after work, slap down the news.

He was bounding up the subway steps like a young

buck when the spinal pinch of a sciatic nerve screamed down into his leg. *Easy, boy, easy.* He winced as he hobbled up and out onto the sidewalk to latch onto a street pole for support. The sign waggled above him, No Parking Tuesdays and Thursdays, but it was Saturday and the panoramic window of a stretch limousine, parked three cars long, made for the perfect mirror. He straightened his bowtie, hand-swept his hair, and walked off the pain, from gimp to limp to an assured stride.

***

Banquet servers milled about the tables. This was in the Sackler Wing at the Metropolitan Museum of Art. There were over a hundred tables, clothed and skirted, around the Temple of Dendur. A sandstone temple with motifs carved into the stones: hieroglyphs, lotus flowers, the sun, the jackal, a bewigged goddess. At the far end of the wing, opposite the temple, stood Egyptian relics and artifacts in front of a long and sleek reflecting pool. It was still an overcast day, a torn patchwork of clouds on display through the western wall, an impressive grid work of windows, possibly over three stories tall with a generous view of Central Park and its autumnal trees. The percussive chatter of wine glasses and silverware being set on the tables continued to echo about the spacious wing.

Jim's positive outlook flat-lined when he saw his tables stationed in the mid-zone. He knew serving his guests two plates at a time would be an out-and-back race-walk from the employee hallway behind the Temple of

Dendur. His wrists already ached, beads of sweat starting to build on his upper lip. His pending fear was that he would blow out his back mid-service. He was place-setting silverware with Nina and Craig, who were both younger than him. Their tables were stationed even further from the employee hallway than his, but their apparent lack of concern about it, helped to relieve some of the stress in his back. He was thinking positive thoughts, *You'll be fine*, and *thankfully there are no stairs to climb*. The slight tremble in his hand appeared to be diminishing as he set the next fork down.

Nina, a muscular and lithe twenty-one, had moved from Oslo to New York to become a model, and Craig, a subdued and pudgy twenty-eight, had moved from Atlanta, Georgia to pursue filmmaking. It astonished Jim that their ages combined exceeded his by a mere five years. Yet they never brushed him off like several of the other servers half his age or younger did. They treated him like a peer.

Nina was more radiant than usual, her straw-blonde hair pulled tightly into a ponytail, her eyes piercingly blue with excitement. She had just landed an ad for West Loop, modeling fleece leggings, which she pretended to do, stopping mid-stride to showcase her tux pant leg, gesturing the length of it with a luxurious sweep of the hand. The pose earned her light applause from Jim and Craig, each tamping a palm with an oversized fistful of silverware. Jim felt inspired to share his news, about his photograph being showcased at a thrift-store opening. Then Craig shared about one of his short films scheduled to screen at an upcoming festival. And they all congratulated each other.

Jim's grin was slowly returning. He polished a fork, set it down, and moved on to the next placement. Then Nina asked Craig where she could see his film. Jim was curious as well, as he polished tines. He had always been silently rooting for Craig, hoping that his flirtations with Nina might evolve into a lasting relationship. The only deterrent Jim could think of was the Pillsbury pudge hinting at Craig's waistline, but he figured Nina might find that cute, knowing beneath it all was a solid man. Then Craig placed a knife on the table to state with casual indifference, "Lincoln Center."

"That's amazing!" Nina hopped and Jim dropped a fork. He swept it up fast, too fast. A sciatic spasm twisted its blade into his back. Happy for Craig, yes! Jim winced as he massaged the pain throbbing in his lower back with the knuckles of his fist. Craig's so young. He could already see him accepting an Oscar, showing it off to the crowd and teleprompters with a triumphant glow. *The fat little shit.*

"Lincoln Center." Nina was still glowing with blush marks on her doll-face cheeks. "And Housing Works." She smiled at Jim, who was polishing a fork faster than usual.

"No," he said, "not Housing Works, but a thrift store like it... in Asheville, North Carolina."

"Nashville?" she said.

"No," Jim said, slipping mid-polish, jabbing tines into his palm.

Craig said, "You mean, ASH-ville?"

Jim nodded, moving onto the next setting.

Craig explained to Nina how Asheville was like Portland, Oregon, only on the east coast.

"Oh," Nina said.

Then Craig added how he and his friends used to frequent Asheville from Atlanta when he was a senior in high school. "It's surrounded by the Blue Ridge Mountains. I mean, they're not the mountains of Norway, but trust me, they're beautiful. The oldest mountains in the world, I think, right Jim?"

"Right," Jim said with a faint smile, continuing to polish forks. The oldest mountains. He strained his eyes as if seeing through a high-altitude mist. There were hemlock trees, diseased and dying, along the Blue Ridge parkway. Some so frail you could kick them, or throw your shoulder into them, to watch them crack and topple to the earth.

"Am I right?" Craig said with a groove-nodding smile. He'd been talking up the corn pudding at 12 Bones in Asheville. Jim had never heard of the barbecue joint, another one of those eateries established after he left, yet he gave the corn pudding the big thumbs up. He almost added Mellow Mushroom to the hype of great eats, biting his lower lip instead, knowing the pizza joint could have closed as long as a decade ago. But he did think of a white lie when Nina asked about his photograph.

He made one up, a silver gelatin print based on a vague memory, three hungover friends, roadside, changing a flat tire to a VW van. There was Sally cranking the jack. Beckah standing there wide-eyed with a tire iron. Ross with a bushy beard, puffing on a cob pipe with a philosopher's frown. He added more to the fabrication, and placed his would-be photograph on display in the trendy French Broad River district, which could end up being true. He described a gentrified textile mill filled with art galleries, a pottery store, upscale antiques ... and soon, he finished saying with a modest flutter of the eyes, his photograph.

"So yeah, it's good." He shrugged. "Though technically not a show. But my photograph will be one of the first things you see when you walk into the store, a massive print on the wall."

Maybe they knew he was pushing it a little, but it didn't matter, because he could see they wanted to be happy for him. Craig even added he'd definitely check it out next time he was in Asheville, a nicety Jim took with a smile, knowing the chances of Craig going to Asheville any time soon were slim to zero. And though there was a bit of a gimp to Jim's approach to the silverware cart, boasting about his photograph had yielded a stride similar to Craig's, one of confidence and purpose, proving that there was more to life than scooping up another fistful of dessert forks. That's when the phone in his pocket buzzed. He'd missed the call. But it was the same number as last night. Jim waggled his phone at Nina and Craig.

"It's about the showing."

He set his forks down. They gave him a good-luck smile. He walked away, pressing the phone to his ear, expecting to hear the husky voice of After Midnight, but it was Ross! And it was so good to hear him: "Whassup, my brother!"... until it wasn't.

Ross's voice was treading into the deep waters of an apology, choppy with cellular static. The Sackler Wing started to blur all around him. The other servers drifted toward obscurity and a distant sarcophagus racked into focus.

Ross continued, "So, I don't know what she told you, but I can guarantee you it's a lie. She has this Delusion of Grandeur thing. It kicks up when she's off her meds. One week she's inviting all her friends to work at an organic farm she's opening, the next it's a microbrewery. It's bad, man, even worse, because I love her... I know you'll love her too when you meet her. You'll see off the bat how her heart's in it, but the rest of her just crumbles sometimes ... Again, I'm sorry. But call me. Really, man, it's been too damn long. I want to know what's going on. So yeah, give me a—"

The voicemail ended there. Jim pocketed the phone and looked at the handful of dessert forks waiting for him back at the table. A streak of sunlight flared off the marble floor. All around him banquet servers continued to set the tables, a dull repetition of wine glasses and silverware being set on white tablecloths. Soon the glare of sunlight vanished from his face and he was left standing there with an overwhelming sadness, not so much for himself, but for Ross and Ross's girlfriend, and the two of them battling it out with her illness. For Jim this was just some shit he'd have to scrape off his shoe. Another one of those moments where you look back at something that could have been. He even managed a smile, reminding himself that this was about a framed print from a moldy old box he had forgotten about, so, no worries, forget the pain, then plop plop, fizz fizz a couple of Alka Seltzers after a long hard scream into a bed pillow.

"You okay?" Craig said.

Jim held up a finger, unable to say more, his eyes welling up with tears. Nina looked concerned too, suggesting he step outside.

"Take in some of that Central Park air," she said with a worried smile.

"Good idea," Jim nodded. Everything he could think, say, or feel was stuck in his throat like a spoonful of shattered glass. He looked to the employee hallway behind the Temple of Dendur, charting his exit, but after passing two tables there was Spencer Donovan in his face, signaling him to stay put. Jim sniffled, holding back the tears.

Spencer was a banquet captain Jim had trained more than five years ago on the basic points of service. Spencer had a flat-top crew cut and the emaciated build of someone who gulps muscle milk and powdered nutrient shakes morning, noon, and night as a supplement to the ultimate workout, eighteen-hour shifts overlooking cater-waiters with a sniper's precision for setting tables and executing five-star points of service.

"Correcting the situation now." He was speaking to the Bluetooth in his ear, noodled with the same fusilli wiring the Secret Service employs. Jim could smell the Binaca on his breath, a noxious spearmint. His patience for Spencer had already eroded. He tried again to edge around him. Spencer signaled again for him to stay put.

What came next was a call to attention for all the servers in the Sackler Wing. Spencer, prodding his forefinger and thumb to his lips, produced a whistle so shrill that several of the servers trotting up to the table had to cover their ears. Nina crossed her eyes and Craig pulled the trigger to a finger gun aimed at his own temple with a head-blown expression. Spencer, standing there as would a master of ceremonies, was waiting for everyone's undivided attention. More than fifty servers shuffled to a standstill around the table. Then Spencer pelted the air of the Sackler Wing with a vital question.

"What is our name?"

"Phenomenal Performance," someone said.

"That's right," Spencer said. "Phenomenal Performance." And then he looked around the table as if to make eye contact with each and every server. "And where does a phenomenal performance begin?"

"With the setting," someone flatly replied.

"That's right," Spencer said, "with the setting." Then he lifted a finger dramatically for everyone to see before he drove it down onto the table where soon the first course would be placed.

"Now I want everyone to look at this setting and tell me if what you see is a Phenomenal Performance."

"Seriously?!" someone said.

"Oh, it's serious." Spencer sharpened his eyes. "And if you don't think it's serious … " He shook his head with disapproval. "Then what are you doing here?"

That's when Jim saw the mistake, knowing Spencer was about to call him out on it. Then someone said, "The dessert fork is backward."

"That's right," Spencer said, spreading all five fingers of his hand onto the edge of the table for emphasis as he continued. "The tines of the dessert fork face east not west at the top of the setting. Now that's a basic point of service, people." Then he stood back from the table, staring prudishly at the dessert fork with disbelief.

"Which means someone wasn't paying attention. Now this is pregame, people, and phenomenal starts with the first step. Someone tripped out of the gate. Would *that* someone like to correct their mistake?" He turned to Jim. "And make it a phenomenal performance."

Jim continued to stare at his mistake on the table, the dessert fork now bigger in his mind than the Temple of Dendur. Then he looked around the table, first at Nina and Craig giving him a sympathetic smile, and then at the assertive faces of future Spencers, along with the rest of the servers who looked bored—one was straining to hide a yawn, others with just-fix-it lazy in their eyes. But it was something more to Jim.

His mistake was being out of touch with Ross for years. His mistake was packing up his ambition, his passion, in contractor bags for the garbage truck. His mistake?... conceding to a lobotomized life of cater-waitering. How many years had he been working for Phenomenal Performance? It was like staring down a blinding white hallway, reminding him that the basic point of service is to never let them know you were ever there. So he reversed the fork, made himself invisible again, and Spencer seemed satisfied. Now everyone could go back to work. Then a smile crept up Jim's face and he switched it back. Made it wrong again.

Someone gasped, "What are you doing?"

Spencer's face hardened.

Everyone was looking at Jim.

He corrected it.

"Finished," Spencer said.

Jim didn't know what he was trying to work out with the fork, but he could feel the confluence of power pivoting one way and then the other every time he turned it. It was just like toggling a switch to a turbine of self-will. Off then on. Off then on. Off then...

"Come on," Craig said, stepping up to Jim. "It's not worth it."

Jim turned from the table to walk away. How many years? The question was still hanging from his face. How many celebrity galas, penthouse buffets, business parties, cruises on the Hudson, ballroom marches? How many years? Had he made it so they never knew he was there? Then he turned around with his arms spread wide, hands ready to flip that table like a sumo wrestler.

"HOW MANY YEARS?!"

But the table never flipped. It did jump, grunting like a donkey, a quarter inch from the floor. A wine glass shattered. But the biggest fall was Jim.

"Give him some room. Give him some room."

Spencer and Craig crouched around him. Time had turned into a dull ringing sound inside Jim's head. Spencer asked if he could move. Everyone had circled around to see Jim on the floor with a blown back.

The pain was still shuddering through him from the neck down, threatening total paralysis. Everyone could see that it was bad. Nina phoned for an ambulance. His right hand was trembling as if trying to grasp onto something. But what he was really attempting to do was point so everyone could see. In the near distance, high above the crowd surrounding him, was a pigeon fluttering in midair. He didn't know how long he watched it, its wings flapping in slow motion.

That would be the picture he would eventually recall from the pained comfort of his sofa, back at his apartment, with a heating pad against the small of his back. That and the look on Nina and Craig's faces when they had turned to glance up at the pigeon. He would have taken a picture of that too, their shared expression as they stood side by side watching the bird swoop down to flap about the Temple of Dendur. Then there was the expression of pity they gave each other before looking again at Jim, who, faint of breath, was still struggling to point toward the pigeon as the paramedics wheeled him out of the Sackler Wing on a gurney.

He could see it all in black and white. A picture taken from the lens of a Nikkormat FT. That would have captured the moment brilliantly. He even imagined pushing the film a stop during development to detail the pigeon and wash out the Temple of Dendur. Who needs the clarity of a temple when you've got a live pigeon?

He was still confused as the paramedics wheeled him up to the ambulance outside the Met. Amid the foot traffic on the sidewalk, he thought he saw Ross leaning against a streetlight pole, with a cracked beer in his hand and a soulful grin. *It's been too damn long.* Jim agreed, knowing soon he would stand again.

JAWBONE ON THE GANGES

The river was polluted with household garbage, candy wrappers, floating idols, scrap metal, burned-out prayer candles. The river was polluted with slaughterhouse slops, factory drainage, colored dyes from a sari mill. The river was polluted with broken furniture, raw sewage, and the ashes and bones of the dead. Women slapped their family laundry dry on the steps of the riverside ghats. Children splashed about with laughter. White-bearded yogis dunked themselves underwater to reappear with serenity in their eyes. For the river was holy, and its believers seemingly immune to the toxicity of its flow.

I wanted to believe. I wanted the faith of someone eager to thrash out into the river Ganges with holy conviction. But I was an outsider looking in—a foreigner, a tourist, midway through a three-month journey to India and Nepal, traveling light with a backpack and a Lonely Planet guidebook. I was scrubbing my teeth with a chew-stick toothbrush I'd purchased from a street vendor.

Sticks, curry, naan, bottled water, chai, fennel-seed candy, I trusted. The overpopulated sidewalks, streets, buses, trains, I trusted too, growing to love the slow crush of being crammed in with the many. There was simplicity in that—to be a singular face in a bodied flow of traffic.

But the river Ganges? My lower intestines cringed. Don't dare touch that water. Side effects could include severe nausea, explosive diarrhea, piercing migraines, rapid hair loss, out-of-body frightmares that have you shaking awake a random cot mate at a youth hostel, imploring them to talk you back down into your skin. These were bullet points of delirium I had already endured on my trip to India and Nepal, except for the rapid hair loss.

This was late October 1995.

I was twenty-five, an American tourist from western North Carolina. "So, you are from the U.S. of A.," was often the greeting from tailors and artisan rug sellers inviting me into their shops with a *come, come* sweep of the arm for chai and English biscuits, or a street-walking beautician inviting me to a park-bench preening, eager to clip my toenails and massage my feet with sandalwood musk, or to scrape clean the innards of my ears with a surgical instrument akin to a darning needle, which I would agree to my final days in India, closing my eyes to the distant song of a gourd-bellied flute wheezing timorously in the open air as the park-bench pro scooped out the ear wax of my travels for a gruesome show and a hasty flick to an Old-Delhi curb.

My ex-girlfriend was in India too. In fact, we were together that day in Varanasi, about to step into a three-person skiff for a boat ride to the funeral pyres, where the flames burn seven days a week, twenty-four hours a day.

I stepped into the boat with a finger hooked in my mouth. Stuck in my teeth was an annoying chew-stick splinter. I couldn't get it out. Simone, in her sun-hat and loose-fitting shirt, seemed bored as she found her seat at the front of the skiff. She'd already been to the funeral pyres. A dull look clouded her hazel green eyes, not so much with a pout, but with the glum assurance of nothing surprising coming anytime soon. Maybe that's what had her nonchalantly letting her fingers trawl through the water as the boatman paddled us into the drift. As if she'd already been anointed by these waters and the black smoke that we were soon to see fuming from the pyres. Morning prayers could still be heard, openly sung from tower windows. The chaotic sound of street traffic grew fainter the further we drifted. I withdrew my finger from my mouth. But the splinter was still there, wedged in the gum line. I continued to tongue at it as I stared downriver, anxious to see the dead.

***

The inspiration for this trip had come from the tail end of a monstrous bong hit, six years earlier, during my college daze in the outskirts of Asheville, North Carolina. My third eye yearned to see more amidst the dorm-room haze that tasted sweetly of red bud and Nepalese hashish smuggled from the stoner squad of students who had just returned from a six-month journey abroad.

India and Nepal had bronzed their flesh and sucked the chub from their faces, bellies, and thighs, and had thickened their eyebrows and toughened their hands. They sat among us in their Hindu wear—saris, dhotis, henna tattoos—a few with red dots centered on their foreheads. All their eyes were heavily lidded and somewhat faded as if having stared too long at a Punjabi sunset. Haley was no longer Haley from Wetumpka, Alabama, but Bahan Haley Sister Hindu. Then there was Brad as Deveena B, Angelo as Gubaara, and Jane as Lolee J. These were nicknames that had been given to them, names that were sure to fade within a month's time, maybe two, before they were once again like every other student on campus.

But that night in Deveena B's dorm room, they had yet to shower since returning from India—smelling less of air travel, and more like the spiced streets of Old Delhi. That alone was enough to cop a buzz. Everyone was seated about the room, either with their legs folded, or on their knees. A pungent warmth emanated from our hosts, comforting as the flames of a mud chulha stove. They were about to bake our minds with stories and gifts from India and Nepal.

Another cough, another bong hit; I continued to stare at the gift that had been unpacked and given to me by Deveena B. I still wasn't sure what to make of it, a dried dung patty braided with thatch for cooking fuel. I wasn't sure if Deveena B had given it to me as a joke. He was always telling me to get my shit together. But the smile he'd given me when presenting the gift with both arms fully extended seemed genuine enough, even when he said it had come from the ass of a holy cow. Then the smoke from someone else's bong hit clouded over me.

Some of their stories were adventurous, like trekking into the Himalayas, or noble, like when they assisted an impoverished family to renovate a shanty wall. There were even more gifts from India to behold, stacked about the room with a cosmic aura: Laxmi Dhoop incense, prayer flags, embroidered shawls, mosaic tapestries, and *chillums*, primitive clay pipes for smoking hash like the sadhus. Most intriguing of all—and not a gift, but one of Deveena B's prized keepsakes—was a *kapala*, a bowl made from a human skull. It was inlaid with tin tamped along the rim with esoteric Sanskrit, a ritual skullcap. This was where Deveena B kept the block of hash, blessing it with quiet intensity every time he plucked a nib for the bong. The more we smoked the more it seemed like we were smoking from the sacred head of death itself. Then someone turned off the festive lighting. Someone else struck up a match. A blue flame fluttered from a monastery oil lamp. Our faces glowed in the dark.

There were other stories too—ones that came with grave and sunken voices. How a fellow student had been hospitalized, believing himself possessed by evil spirits in Gujarat. Or how another student claimed to have several out-of-body experiences. Or how Gubaara had woken more than once several blocks from his hostel cot with his head on the lap of a Bade Baba statue.

"That happened in two different cities," he said, "Two!" emphasizing the fact with a show of two fingers. Spooky shit, no doubt. There seemed to be more to say, and not just about Gubaara Angelo's story. But it was more than they were willing to share, except between themselves with cryptic smiles, as if they'd each returned with a spiritual puzzle piece of their own—that only by having been there could one *begin* to comprehend. That was what had me gnawing on a hangnail in the lamp-lit dark, thinking, "Man, I've *got* to go to India."

This was also where I'd met Simone, who was there like me for the kapala smoke-out and to hear everyone's stories. Before the festive lighting had turned off, we had glanced at one another from across the room a couple of times. Her hair was chopped short and messy, dyed peroxide blonde. She wasn't a Goth, though her skin was a shade shy of deathly pale. She was the only one on campus who consistently wore black on black with purple socks brimming from her blueberry Doc Marten boots. The same boots she was stepping back into as I laced up my sneakers in the hallway after the smoke-out.

We continued the discussion of our classmates' trip on a wooded footpath between dorms—India, Nepal, clarified butter, a *gompa* monastery in Ladakh. Even the proboscis of Ganesh, and what it would be like to ride bareback on an elephant as Bahan Haley Sister Hindu had done. Simone said she would go one day. I said, in a flaky sort of way, that I would too. But I could see from her determined look that she was going.

Then she left and I continued to stare at the empty space where she'd been standing. I was too high to even recall her saying goodbye. Down the steep path was the crosswalk over the main road to the other side of campus.

But I'd wandered into the woods, to find myself standing in a patch of dead wet leaves among tall, dark trees. I was thinking about the kapala and the Sanskrit inlaid on the rim of the skull, and Deveena B when he tilted his braided goatee toward the kapala to say that that was where we were all headed. A truth pretty much anyone understands as soon as they're old enough to realize what it means to be alive. That one day you'll be dead. But the kapala and the Sanskrit... there was something *more* than just death.

That's when the ground jumbled out from under me like after having a branch snag your foot mid stride. I wasn't sure if I was falling or levitating, but I was reaching for a place to land. Maybe even shouting silently, as one would in outer space. *How old is the oldest language and who was first to tamp Sanskrit onto a plated skull, words that translate into something like...*

I don't know what.

I was out in the road, shielding my eyes. Oncoming headlights swerved around me. I could have been struck dead. The blaring horn of the VW van followed me all the way back to my dorm. There was dirt in my mouth and a yellow birch leaf stuck to my lips. I shut the room door. Then I shut the closet door. I settled on a mound of dirty laundry. Never has the stink of crusty socks been so refreshing. Empty coat hangers loomed overhead. I sat there, nursing on a brick of cheddar cheese, or had it been the dung cake?

Then I dropped out of college.

I didn't see Simone again until the following year at a Jesus Lizard concert at the Cat's Cradle in Chapel Hill. She had dropped out too. We were in the thick of the crowd, surging toward the stage. The lead singer, David Yow, was barefoot and drunk in oil-stained jeans. He was stumbling between the speaker stacks as one would on a passenger ship about to capsize. He snaked the mic cord round his neck with lunacy bulging in his eyes. The music thundered on as he snarled into the mic.

The front of the crowd pushed up against the stage and the mosh pit widened into a frenzy. I had lost Simone and was looking for her when someone shoved me into the pit. She came crashing into view. All I could do was brace myself. Then we spastically danced as we threw each other about the pit, freely stomping and kicking like everyone else. We were in love.

***

Five years later, we broke up—shortly after being inoculated for our trip to India. I don't blame her today for her betrayal, sleeping with someone else. I had been the first to leave, emotionally abandoning her a year before. I could blame my alcoholism, puking on her side of the bed more than once, or the morning I forgot to take off from work, when she drove herself to the abortion clinic, as reasons why the last two years of our relationship downshifted into celibacy, where we continued to share the electric bills, toothpaste, and a French press. Then she moved out, a couple of months before we left for India. Our plans split into separate flights with separate itineraries. But we did agree to meet midway on our own separate trips, never to discuss her infidelity, or what her new lover might think of our meeting in India.

It didn't matter because wherever we went he was always there, an invisible man wedged between us, a soft-spoken architect, some wanker named Michael, who I had only met once under the seething pretense of whooping his ass, which I backed down from doing, though I did wake him up, rocking his Airstream trailer with drunken powers. He and Simone popped out of the pod of moonlit aluminum with matching bedheads, looking more bemused than threatened as I continued to seethe with satanic blather I'd picked up from a used occult paperback. If a mere tenth of the chthonic blight had landed then it would have been hives for Michael and a prolific yeast infection for Simone. But in the moment, it was nothing more than an impotent spittle of rage, and a machine-gun rattle of gravel against Michael's trailer from the spinning rear wheels of my Honda Civic as I drove off, beating my knuckles bloody against the dash.

He was a career man, older and sophisticated, yet with a rugged appeal, a man with slender hands who knew how to swirl a wine glass before approving the first sip. Simone was a baker in a small mountain town café, an hour's drive east from our remote cottage in western North Carolina, and a two-block walk from Main Street where Michael spent his weekdays laboring over blueprints for geodesic domes and ergonomic bungalows, while no doubt building an appetite for an afternoon slice of Simone's spice cake with lemon iced tea.

My life was managing frankfurters at a hot-dog stand

on the Nantahala River. I had no ambition. I often referred to this period as my early retirement with a fun-job on the side, slinging chili dogs to kayakers and families on the Nantahala for a rip-roaring good time. Yeah, I was slacking-off my twenties, and looking back I'd do it again. It's just where I was then, and now I see it as a privilege, absolutely—the average day's wage in India is less than what you'd pay for a chili-dog combo with crinkle-cut fries, but who's to say that a tour-guide boatman on the river Ganges isn't slacking his life off too.

The one Simone and I eventually rode with that day in Varanasi seemed to have the same cooked-out serenity in his eyes as several of the lifers river-guiding on the Nantahala. Those Nantahala grinners, in it for the rip of the rapids and the glistening song of the river. It was simple living, and maybe that's always been my great aspiration, though the pain of an odd-job resumé will eventually catch up to you, wake you up in the middle of the night, whisper all kinds of hate-speech about what your life should have been.

But back in the hot-dog days it was about lacing up my hiking boots to mosey on the Appalachian trail, or honk the hours away on an alto sax or bass clarinet, improvised ditties I'd recorded on a portable tape deck that upon recent review sounded like wounded dogs. That's probably why I didn't weep when I pawned off the horns for additional funds to swing the trip to India. The rest of the travel money came from a windfall check from G-Ma and G-Pa.

I'd like to say I worked hard saving up for India; it's possible I even said that to some of my friends, but pumping cheese on nachos and chili dogs was just enough to cover rent and the weekly Jim Beam. I will say there were shifts when the line cramped up at the window and you had to whisk up a ten-gallon drum of powdered cheese. That was hard work. You'll break a sweat doing that—appeasing hungry faces on a food break from a Tweetsie railroad tour on the Nantahala Gorge, a break that would always come with a combative scramble of hairy dad-hands for the next chili dog, and children pawing, "Mine! Mine! Mine!"

***

I'm not sure whose idea it was for us to meet during our own separate trips. But I do remember that when we finally met, the air between us was platonic. Sure, we were excited to see each other—with big smiles and a soulful hug, but beyond that it seemed we were nothing more than just two friends who had happened to cross paths while traveling abroad. This was in a border-town tea-house in Nepal. We were recounting our own separate travels, in part to determine what we would do together.

The chai came in a flimsy plastic cup. Every sip left the roof of my mouth tasting as if I'd licked a vinyl record. I studied the print on the side of the cup. *Please deform before disposal.* I guess they didn't want the cups to get reused. I thought about mentioning it after finishing my chai, when Simone said she'd already been to the funeral pyres. I crushed my cup single-handedly. A streak of chai slid down the length of my forearm. She seemed surprised that I hadn't already been to the pyres. I told her I thought it was something we were going to do together. I continued to stare at the corner of the table.

She said, "We never agreed to that," which was true. "But I'll go again if you want."

She reached across the table for my hand. I pulled back to wipe the chai from my arm on my cargo shorts. It was a drag, feeling she had already "done" Varanasi, the river Ganges, and the funeral pyres. But I said, "Yeah, let's do it."

And it was where we went first after crossing the border into India. But the feeling never left, like watching a movie with someone who's already seen it—you can't help but feel they're always a scene or two ahead of you. So no matter where the boatman took us that day there would be no catching up to Simone on the river Ganges.

He invited us into his three-person skiff and started paddling us out into the current of the dark green water. He was bony with a wooden face, his eyes sunk under wiry brows, his hair swept over his head, a thick oily sheen. He was wearing a *dhoti*, a thong akin to a cloth diaper, his footwear cut from the worn rubber of a radial tire. Each stroke came with a harder push. Certitude was in the depths of his filmy eyes. I suddenly felt a twinge of panic. We weren't going where we should be going. He was ferrying us across the river.

"Shouldn't we be headed downriver?" I said.

"Number two," he said with another deep stroke of the paddle. "Then funeral pyre."

I didn't know what he was talking about, or where he

was going. There was nothing ahead of us, except for a sandbar, wide as a fifty-acre slab of Punjabi desert.

"Where's he taking us?" I asked Simone.

She didn't know or seem to care.

"It's not like we have a ten o'clock reservation we can't break at the funeral pyre." She stared out at the water. "Just relax."

So, I sat with myself. The boatman was still bobbling his head with a confident grin, as if "number two" was some great destination every tourist had to see. Well, I didn't want to see it, so I waved my arms, flagging my hands back and forth.

"Number two! Not necessary!"

Snorting up a mouthful of phlegm, he ignored me and spat into the river as we swiftly approached the sandbar. The nose of the skiff beached upright. He plunked knee-deep into the water, and rushed up to the beach. He dragged the boat from the bow, pulling it further onto the sand. Then he promised to return shortly before sprinting into the distance. I spanked a horsefly dead on my arm and flicked it into the frothy scum line of water.

Simone had already stepped out of the boat to wander along the shore. The boatman was out on the horizon of sand. As I watched him squat, the meaning of number two became perfectly clear. From the sound of his grunting, I figured we would be there awhile.

It seemed Simone had discovered something. She never looked back to see if I was joining her. I stepped out of the boat with a clumsy misstep, dunking mid-calf into the scummy shallows... *fuck.*

I shook the water from my sandal as I walked away from the skiff. There were no signs of life on this vast sandbar, except for a distant flock of seagulls squabbling with each other and another troubled grunt from the boatman. It was strange, almost ominous, to be somewhere so completely isolated, juxtaposed to the rowboats and barges on the river, and the bathers at the ghats, with the city backdrop of saffron-and-almond colored buildings and bulbous-and-ornate temple spires, some possibly as old as the rising sun.

Why were we alone? This seemed like a great place for relaxation. Why weren't there any beach chairs, or family reunions, or kids chasing after each other in a spirited game of tag—*you're it!* But we weren't the only ones on this sand bar. That's when I found myself beside Simone, taking in the view at our feet—a human corpse, fully decomposed to a skeletal state. We both just stood there, solemn with awe.

The skull was agog and tilted back, as if somewhere up above, beyond the morning sun gently baking our backs, was something to behold—as if there, all great mysteries might finally come to an end.

***

To escape the cyclical bondage of reincarnation, Hindus strive for *moksha*—a celestial state of perfection wherein the soul is freed into the cosmos. There is no better place to strive for moksha than the funeral pyres in Varanasi—where the deceased are swaddled in white cloth for public cremation.

Not everyone is allowed this funerary rite; eligibility for the pyre belongs only to those of a certain caste, a system one is born into. Those born into the lowest caste, known as Untouchables, are ineligible for cremation. They cannot be ceremoniously buried, or buried at all. It's not uncommon for street sweepers to serve as undertakers for Untouchables, releasing their bodies into the river Ganges, sometimes with a flat stone bound to their chests to weigh them down to the river-bottom, or sometimes bound to nothing at all, with the flow of the current leading them downriver and eventually out to sea. Or, in this case, to the opposing shore.

A gust of wind stirred across the sand. How many bodies were half-buried or scattered on this sandbar? And those weren't seagulls in the near distance, but raw-headed vultures, there to feed off some other carcass too far away to identify as man or beast. And what of the corpse at our feet? I might have taken it more seriously had there been more than just bones, ligature, and rib-cage tufts of sun-cured meat.

The breeze was persistent enough for Simone to keep her hand on her sun hat, with its floppy brim riffling. She was still pondering the corpse, more with a detached grin than sympathy for the dead. It seemed almost make-believe, like a jump-scare skeleton you'd expect on a haunted-house ride, or like the prop skeleton that used to hang from the back rack in Ms. Dorsett's science class. Maybe that's why I toed at the skull, first nudging the temple then the jawbone, which came unhinged with surprising ease. Suddenly there it was—a human jawbone on the sand.

"That's a keeper," Simone said.

Or maybe she didn't, but let's say she did, because

I still don't want to accept what follows as my own transgression. Had she never been there, I still wonder if I would have rummaged through my day bag for a handkerchief to pick up the jawbone. Was I doing this to impress her? To bring back the days we used to sit around her stereo, listening to Saint Vitus, Agnostic Front, or one of her more treasured albums, a clear vinyl print of *Lie: The Love and Terror Cult* by Charles Manson.

We had shared many a bottle of blood-red gallon wine listening to a shaggy-haired Manson butcher chords on acoustic guitar while crooning "Home Is Where You're Happy". We smoked Nat Sherman pastel-colored cigarettes while watching vintage horror films from bed, *Carnival of Souls* on VHS, or *Night of the Living Dead*. I always think of the boyfriend creeping out from behind a tombstone to taunt his girlfriend. "They're coming to get you Barbara. They're coming to get you." Now I was coming to get Simone. Call it slacker black magic, or spontaneous necromancy, or a hasty grab to raise the dead of our courtship days.

I know I shouldn't have picked it up, but it was thrilling to hold. The hairs on my arms stood upright.

"How is it something so dead can make you feel so alive?"

She ignored my question, but said, "That would make a great gift."

I was bending the bone, surprised by how pliable it was—like rubber. I expected it to be more brittle, like a wishbone, like maybe it would crack in half—and you know the wish. It did feel like it was coming true when Simone's arm brushed up against mine.

"Who will you give it to?" she said, already assuming

I would give it away, forgetting my collection of sun-bleached bones from various vermin and birds on the windowsill in what used to be *our* living room. But she was right, this was too good to keep. I even recalled how much it would have blown my mind if Deveena B. had given me the kapala instead of giving me that dried patty of dung. He didn't even give a shit about that kapala, leaving it on a dorm-room shelf to collect dust, next to a sherbet-orange guitar pick he'd nabbed from the stage of a Grateful Dead show in Kentucky. Gifts from someone else have more power than the gifts we give ourselves. I could already see this jawbone being proudly displayed on someone's wall. I just had to give it to the right friend.

And we reviewed a list of friends, my friends, who used to be *our* friends—the friends I would see first upon returning from India, starting with Ross, a failed blacksmith turned Ramada-Inn front-desk concierge, who'd probably say, "Get that fucking thing away from me."

"True." Simone tittered and I paused to look back from where we had left the skeleton, to take a mental snapshot, not of the corpse, but the trail of our footprints in the sand. I imagined how I would share this image with her years later, telling her, *That's when I knew we were getting back together.*

It was just one of those moments we've all had: you want to believe, only to find that crystal ball again someday, half shattered and full of sand. But it was my moment, my time to believe, as I wrapped the jawbone up into a red bandana, stuffing it inside the thigh pocket of my cargo shorts.

Then there was one friend, we fiendishly agreed, who

no doubt would be filled with morbid glee if given a human jawbone from India. I could already see it on display above the entryway to his bedroom, or tacked to the wall like a side note to an atomic blast among the many off-kilter posters of Earache bands: Bolt Thrower, The Entombed, Brutal Truth.

The boatman glared at me with disapproval as we stepped up to the skiff. His eyes narrowed over the bulge in the thigh pocket of my cargo shorts. How could he have known? He'd been too far away to see me take it. It wasn't easy to ignore the disapproval knotted on his brows. I almost lost my balance. Stepping into the boat, I had to latch onto the gunwale with both hands before taking my seat.

"Very bad," he said as he pushed the skiff off shore and clambered up into the boat. Water dripped from his knees as he plonked down onto the stern bench. "Very, very bad," he said again with a deep backward stroke to turn us around.

Simone looked at me. "What's he talking about?"

"I don't know, the weather?" I shrugged, signaling with a tilt of the chin toward the bulge in my thigh pocket.

"Oh," she sighed with a soft smile. Then that was that. Nothing else was said and we kept our backs to the boatman as he continued to paddle. There it was—the holy river Ganges. The late-morning sun glittered on the water. What does holy even mean, anyway? Did I know, back then?

We were both just kids in our mid-twenties, to say nothing of the disregard I had for the jawbone I'd pilfered. How such a discovery could have made me feel so high, I don't know. It's still something I think about, and how it never crossed my mind that day to think of the skeleton in the sand as having once been an actual person, or to think of the life they had lived—the worries, doubts, triumphs, and sorrows they had had and hopefully overcame. No, for me that day it was the ultimate of tourist finds, ghoulishly abuzz with magical properties, or so I thought, believing it had imbued me with some mystical magnetism just by being in my pocket. So, would I smack that guy who took the jawbone upside the head today? I'm not sure, but I certainly wouldn't give him a high five.

**

Then, as quick as a finger snap, it was my last day traveling with Simone. Her trip was set to continue indefinitely. Mine was coming to an end. I had run out of money, with an emergency family loan getting me through the last third of my trip. Plus, it had never come up between us, the idea that we might continue to travel together. The most we had shared on our travels was garlic naan and a queen-sized bed, one night in Agra, the only night she ever brought up Michael. I slept fully clothed, facing the wall.

Our last day had been in Jodhpur, the blue city of Rajasthan. A maze of claustrophobic walkways and sudden open plazas. Blue-concrete buildings, some were faded, and others chipped. These buildings had been painted blue for psychological reasons, to make you believe that somewhere nearby is an ocean with its waves waiting to crash over you. But beyond the city's perimeter is nothing but desert sand, miles of it, except for Jodhpur's main attraction—the Mehrangarh Fort. You can see it from the blue-city streets, crowning a sheer-faced, rocky outcrop, with palaces which are now museums rising from behind the fortress wall. A wink of sunlight shimmered from one of its many turrets.

We had skipped touring the Mehrangarh Fort that day for a camel-ride trek to a Jain temple. Upon entering, my palms turned sweaty. There were sultry goddesses everywhere, full-bodied sculptures on the inner walls and curved ceilings, each one wide-hipped with a buxom rack of immortal breasts and nipples pert as sandstone darts. These goddesses were warriors too, each one with eight to twelve arms wielding scimitars, daggers, tridents, and other head-lopping, heart-lancing instruments of terror. My eyes kept stealing back to the bodice of each one. A sick, delicious feeling stirred in my groin. Just to suckle on those rock-solid breasts would have been worth decapitation. Outside, I gulped my water ration dry, letting it overflow down my chin and shirt.

The aggressive heat of the day and the surrounding desert started to sound like a swarm of bees. Maybe a flesh-eating assault of locusts was on the way. The remainder of our camel-riding trek out of the Thar desert was one long, dehydrated jaunt into the blazing white eye of the sun.

Camels don't trot, they gallop, and my ability to walk afterward had been impaired. I was stiff in one leg, with a dull pain stabbing into the small of my back with every other step. The camel I'd ridden had been cantankerous, busting my ass with its hump the entire time. Simone's camel had appeared to maintain a much gentler gait. She even seemed tickled from the afternoon trek. If I could have just given her a shard of my discomfort. I needed a painkiller, or some aspirin, as we continued our walkabout through the blue-city streets of Jodhpur. Dusk was on the horizon, bruised clouds in a pinkish sky.

We entered a street market. I followed her into the shade of a canopy tent. There was a variety of spices in wide-open sacks of burlap—fenugreek, tamarind, dill seed, turmeric. She lifted a piece of star anise to my nose.

"Smells like licorice, right?" I nodded yes and she smiled. But the ability to smell had been drubbed out of me. She could sense it too, asking if I was okay. I told her I was fine, but the pain was still in my back. I needed to keep walking it off. I left her with the spices. Moments later a vendor dressed as a hermetic holy man invited me to his table. The smile of eternal wisdom in his eyes seemed to suggest the baked goods on the wobbly card table before him had been blessed by Hindu gods, and not the ones waiting to lambast the world with catastrophic powers, but the ones radiating with serenity—those care-free gods, the originators of the man-bun hairdo, mellowed out with lazy lidded eyes, blue skins with a weightless ease about them, as if to say there is nothing to life but to merely float, and float you shall. The sadhu's grin remained tranquil and inviting.

"Hash brownies," he said.

The edibles on the sheet pan were cracked and dry as square cuts of dung. Suddenly I was transported back to my dorm-room closet, the night I'd spent glazed in a hash-induced death sweat. I should have passed with a simple "thanks, but no thanks." But the vendor's smile elevated my mood. He even said, "One-hundred percent good time." Could it be possible? To go back to that feeling I had the first time I ever smoked hash. I was alone in a grassy pasture, where I stretched out on my back to look up at the clouds. They were soft as pillows and I could have watched them pass for an eternity. Then the brownie sadhu thanked me for my purchase. He raised his hands in prayer to the symbol on his forehead. It looked like a tuning fork, finger painted white, flaking at the edges. I could already hear the ping of a two-pronged note, the promise of its frequency cleansing the air around me. I returned the thanks with prayer hands of my own.

I hadn't even conferred with Simone before making this purchase, telling myself it was just one brownie. I started to head her way, where she was perusing a stand of alien fruits and root vegetables. It just felt right. I also thought it would be good for my back. I stood there midstream in the flow of the street-market crowd as they shuffled past me, women in saris, men in turbans, boys darting about barefoot in dress shirts and trousers, their bodies brushing against mine, a shove here, a push there.

Is there any way to make a connection with India beyond being jostled by throngs of locals, or the consumer transaction of buying this or that, or going into another temple of a religion you don't understand? Maybe that's what I was hoping for, a connection, as I peeled the wax paper from the treat in my hand, wanting the brownie to lead the way. I could already hear the screen door clapping shut behind my inner child, with chocolate crumbs on his lips, rushing out into the afternoon with nothing to do but play.

The last time I smoked hash was with a rickshaw driver I had befriended in Mumbai. This was a few weeks before I met up with Simone. After I smoked up with the driver, he took me to a bar with a dirt floor and sheet-metal walls. A carpet-dealer friend of his escorted me to a corner table. It was covered with peanut shells that he swept clean with his arm. It was a table for high-standing stools, but there were no stools, so we stood there. Then the rickshaw driver arrived with three beers in wooden mugs insisting the far right one was mine. It looked no different from the other two frothy ales. I figured they were out to drug me, steal my passport, traveler's checks, everything, even my clothes. I'd heard such stories, scary "traveler bewares" from other tourists—how you could wake up ass-naked with nothing but the desert and non-English speaking villages all around you. *No money, no ID, who then will you be?* The rickshaw driver and the carpet-dealer continued to stare at me pensively, the dealer with red, betel-nut teeth and black-dyed eyebrows, the driver tapping his hand beside my beer.

"Drink. Drink. This is best beer in all of India."

The hash had slowed the clock, sharpened my hearing too, his hand slowly booming with every tap on the table, the expectant grin on his face waiting for me to take the first sip. I was the only tourist in the bar, possibly the only tourist in this entire district.

"Nope, I'm fine."

I stiffened upright, suddenly speaking louder than everyone in the room. I told them I had to piss, which could have been anywhere on the floor. It was that kind of bar. Then I shoved my way outside, the wafer sheet-metal door yawned wide, stayed wide, and I kept on walking, sensing them behind me, reaching to lure me back inside.

I started to run.

It could have been a premium beer they were offering me, and nothing but a premium beer. If so, I hope he enjoyed it down to the last sip. This was one of the problems I had in India, feeling disconnected from the culture and its people. When I did try to cross that barrier I often felt any friendliness I encountered was because they saw me only for my money, or to entice me into making money with them as their American connection to sell carpets and souvenirs.

From this I had developed a general distrust, that anyone reaching for my hand in India was simply doing so to guide me toward something I should purchase, or toward some unbelievable business opportunity. But the brownie sadhu guiding me to his edibles seemed a kind man, like he'd made them as a gift for anyone and everyone. I don't know, maybe I was just tired and sweaty and thought it might help with the pain in my back.

"What's that?" Simone said as we left the street market.

I offered her some, after gagging lightly on the first bite.

"Hash brownie."

She declined, seeing how shitty it tasted from the look on my face.

"Sure?" I shouted over a diesel rickshaw buzzing past us up the road.

"Maybe later," she shouted back.

That was enough to save a couple of bites, and ball them back up into the wax paper with an unsteady hand. We were headed back to the hotel, a room with twin beds, where we would rest a while, before deciding where to eat dinner. There was a goat curry place Lonely Planet raved about. But I would have to act as if I'd discovered it somehow on my own. Simone thought relying on Lonely Planet cheated the experience of traveling. She never wanted to admit she was a tourist, traveling more as an expat than as someone visiting India. She dressed local too, that evening in a plain-weave shirt, collarless and cambric gray, untucked over the hips of her gauze-brown pants and sandals, giving her a drab and genderless look. Her hair was chopped short, untended, the color of trampled straw.

She had left the Simone behind who had lived in North Carolina, the one who used to dye her hair peroxide blonde, puff on Nat Sherman cigarettes, and play with fake intestines. But she kept her stiff-backed posture, looking at me as an expat would a tourist. That was the distance I felt between us, and what it was saying was that she *was* in India. Me? I was just visiting.

Though now looking back, I know she was probably just as lost as I was, only better at hiding it, yielding an aura of self-assurance, one of belonging to the labyrinthine hold of India. But looking beneath it all, there was also a young American hot to shed her suburban roots for the smug appeal of eternal wisdom gained from flitting about India, getting a suntan while breathing in the smells of anise, fenugreek, saffron, and the diesel stink of another rickshaw buzzing up the road.

But soon my mild resentment toward her lifted, along with the pain in the small of my back. The brownie was beginning to work its magic. The slow burn of dusk glimmered on the street. Every breath felt cinematic. If I could just keep it at this level I figured I would be fine, but that's the problem with hash brownies. There's no controlling how high you'll go, or how fast you'll come down. You just have to have faith it'll be alright, trust the mural of Shiva winking at you from a blue wall, or tune in to the playful spirit of children challenging each other to a handstand, a girl walking on her hands with her legs bent overhead, the others pointing at her in awe.

The streets in India are always pulsing with life. It's kinetic, an electrical charge, one you persistently strive to catch, becoming addicted to it. I shimmied my hands together, going with the first song that jangled into my mind, thinking Simone would chime in—a song "our boy" Charlie Manson liked to sing.

But she maintained a bemused distance, as one would with their ex fumbling to revive the mojo that had once been between them. I lurched ahead so I could turn around and strut backwards while giving her a whiny serenade.

"Garbage dump, garbage dump, Oh, *whyyyyy*, do they call me a garbage *duuuuump?*"

But you could see it in her eyes, even with the dying light of day on her face, she wasn't shutting me out, but she wasn't letting me in either. Maybe it was because she knew within the hour I'd be too baked to even mutter a single word. Hell, I wouldn't even make it to goat curry, or any dinner. I'd be lost within myself, on a bed of my own, face to face with the cracks in the wall, clutching the pillow as one would a life preserver. That was how far this brownie was about to kick my fucking ass. But before that happened we stopped outside our hotel.

It was a three-story building that stood at a slight lean. There were no more than ten rooms. Our room was at the back of the third floor. There was no one outside the Blue Hotel, except for a sacred cow. It wasn't uncommon for holy cows to be left unattended to wander the streets of India. This one had a long and decorative blanket draped over its back. It was standing there, with subdued eyes, as if tuning in to the distant bells of Nirvana. All I could do was cup my hands to my mouth as Simone stepped up to the cow. She gave it a sensuous hug around the neck and whispered into its ear, which fluttered from whatever she'd said. Then she goaded me to do the same, adding, "Don't forget to make a wish."

A wish? I thought... *For what? For me? For us? Oh, just make a wish, any wish when hugging a sacred cow. That's just what you do.* I swatted at a house fly that had buzzed off the cow's ear. All I could think was that this might be the cosmic endorsement I was searching for to boost my brownie high to the next level. Forget the belly full of dread I'd had earlier in the day, when I'd approached the camel, which had seemed to want to spit in my face, while the guide struggled to keep him restrained. I approached this holy cow with open arms, as if to embrace whatever benevolence the universe had to offer. I could feel the warmth of its breath on my hand as I reached forward to whisper... what? I still can't recall.

Then suddenly I was over ten feet tall, grappling midair with confusion, as the ground rushed against my back. There was nothing to do but grab at the air, as if I would find my next breath there, or at least the strength to stand again. The fact was still dawning on me that I had just been head-butted by a holy cow.

What was it about me that seemed so threatening? The question continued to ache inside my ribs. I dusted myself off after standing with trembling legs.

There was a feeling that had been building this entire trip, a feeling that I belonged neither here nor anywhere else, that the universe was simply tolerating me. I think I sucked my thumb to sleep that night, too dehydrated to wet the bed. I did see the boatman paddling his skiff through the black waters of my mind. "Very bad," he kept saying again and again. Was this karmic retribution for my stealing the jawbone? The ceiling started to lower over me as would the lid of a coffin. I'm not even sure what Simone did with the rest of her night.

The following morning was goodbye.

We shared a tender hug, my ribs still aching, my back still stiff, the impact of the holy cow's head still lodged in my chest, accompanied by the memory of that desert camel hissing at me, a menagerie of India and all its wildlife eager for me to leave. Simone may have also said, "Take care of yourself." Or something unnerving like that. I didn't even bother to ask where she was going next. What I remember most was the red dust blooming from the back-end of the open-air jeep. The suspension was shot too, the road rough and uneven. You had to hold tight. There was a couple sitting across from me, lovers from Australia. Every time the jeep jostled hard enough for us to hop from our seats they glommed onto each other, deliriously giddy as idiots on a carnival ride.

How I wished they would just buck off the jeep, but it never happened.

Yet, I continued to force myself to watch the red dust as it swirled down the road. You could still see the blue city shimmering in the distance. Then it was gone and so was Simone. I wiped the sweat from my palms across the thighs of my cargo shorts. Then I held my own hands, squeezing one more tightly than the other. The road and the desert continued to rattle all around me like an earthquake.

Hours later I found a seat on an Old Delhi rooftop among an odd assortment of plastic chairs. There was no one else there. The view at the roof's edge overlooked the narrow street below. There was a row of bridal shops next to an electrical repair shop. I was sitting beside a claw-foot bathtub. It was smoking with red-hot coals, there as a bug-deterrent. I was going to miss India, still feeling that there was much, much more to see. A breeze shoved the smoke into my face, stinging my eyes. I kept them wide open.

***

Buzzers, bells, rickshaws, bicycles, the tinny honking of demanding taxis, this sounded less like constrained traffic than an automotive wall of chaos junking up onto the store-front window of the travel agency. The waiting room could use a good ironing too; the laminate floor and wood-paneled walls were bubbled and warped. The humidity was so oppressively thick that you could suck it up with a straw. Everyone was oozing with sweat, there with their suitcases, backpacks, and carry-on luggage. I wiped my forehead with a bandana. We were all tourists, waiting for the shuttle bus to take us to the airport.

There was an industrial fan that was simply moving the heat around the room. The four-foot pole was corroded with rust. The guard rail was missing and the exposed blades were whirling dangerously fast. The fan was wobbling like a death threat. If it did fall, maybe I'd play savior, keep it from landing on the couple seated next to it—let the blades chop at my arms. I can't say I was looking forward to going home.

Delhi to Bahrain to London to New York to Charlotte, North Carolina, that was my flight path—four planes, twenty-two hours, should everything go without delay. There was the issue, too, of the intestinal bug now traveling with me. I thought I had crapped things out to completion last night, but there was still a colonic rumble raring for an encore. I clenched my teeth, waiting for the threat to pass.

There was no one sitting at the information desk, and behind it on the wall was a row of scenic posters, one of which was dangling from a single strip of tape. But all the other posters were still hanging on strong—the Taj Mahal, the Himalayas, a Goa beach party. Then there was the tangerine skyline of Varanasi—a thatched roof fishing boat on the river Ganges. My mouth turned sticky, my eyes burned. I looked down at my backpack and unbuckled the lid and rummaged inside. I still had it with me—the jawbone.

It was poorly wrapped in a crumpled wad of newspaper. I studied the newsprint, the ornate characters of The Hindu language. It was pleasing to the eye as calligraphy, and yet indecipherable—a guilty reminder that English was my first and only language. I could feel the shape of the jawbone through the paper. My fingertips were stained with newsprint. Was I really going to bring this back to America?

The couple nearest me smelled of coconut oil and sandalwood, and I wondered if they could smell the fear on me. I whiffed at one of my own armpits. But no one was paying attention to me.

A group of Germans had perked up. They were listening to their friend. In a sweat-stained Havana hat, he was effusively speaking to them. It seemed he was recounting some highlight from their trip. Then he winced and they gasped as he started to scrub his hands like he couldn't clean them fast enough. This must've been the climax of his story. Then he freed his hands and his friends erupted with laughter. So whatever the story had been—it seemed, a mess encountered, a mess resolved.

What would I tell customs? That I'd picked this up in some art fair in Jaisalmer or Tamil Nadu? I had, in a panic last night, thought to glue some fake jewelry onto the jawbone. The plan was to make it pretty as a sacred gift. I only got as far as gluing a plastic ruby on the back of my hand to test the strength of the rubber cement before the door crashed open. A fantastic hallucination. The boatman was rushing toward me, to beat me with his paddle. I think that's when the shits had me sprinting for the bathroom. *You can't take this to America!*

Another colonic rumble yanked at my bowels. There was no bathroom in the travel agency. I thought I was passing out, because the room had turned dark, but it was a power outage. Slowly the industrial fan wobbled to a standstill. The room was now two shades darker than the light of day outside. The group across from me appeared unfazed, continuing their conversation. But I was fidgeting in my seat, trying to sit just right to stop the colonic spasm from erupting, or maybe it had.

Then with a sudden electrical hum, the power came back on. The fan chirped back to life, wobbling its heavy head. The gap-toothed German was convulsing with laughter again. That's when I stood up to check my rear end, gently touching my shorts, sensing more swamp ass than an actual blow out.

I looked down at the jawbone, loosely clutched in its packaging, on the chair. Here I was alone. No Simone. No magic. Whatever necrotic spark there'd been, had gone. And as to giving the jawbone to a bro? I had picked up several packs of Monkey Boy bidis, the poor man's cigarette, what the Untouchables smoke. I'd just stick to passing those out to my friends. They wouldn't get us high, but we would all certainly share a cough.

I stepped up to the information desk as if to peruse the wire rack of travel brochures. I had the package in my hand. When the shuttle bus arrived, I bent forward as if to retrieve something from under the desk.

Then I returned to my chair to hoist my backpack onto my shoulders. It was still a heavy load. I never looked back as I stepped out into the dusty light of day.

The ride to the airport was surprisingly smooth. It took three matches to get a bidi lit. I coughed after the first puff.

Festive music played from the dash—synth horn and tabla, a woman's pleasing voice. We passed a five-story hospital and an ambulance sped out of the lot with its sirens on. I was thinking about what I'd left behind. My hand was trembling as I took another puff. It'll always be there, at least in my mind, there in the foot well, beneath the desk of travel brochures. Things to do in India.

ABOUT THE AUTHOR

For years, Ian hosted a book club at a pizzeria in Greenwich Village, New York, dubbed The Rivoli Institute of Pizza and Literature. There he studied masterworks of fiction, miraculously not once staining a page with marinara sauce—okay, maybe once, but it was a Harry Crews book, and he would have approved. Ian's also been a member of several other reading groups at the Center for Fiction and with other friends. He's also a graduate of the CUNY BA program in Fiction, a student alum from The Writers Studio, and former member of several writing workshops in DUMBO, Prospect Heights, and Williamsburg, Brooklyn. He's also a crude-animator, voice-over artist, documentarian, musician and video editor. Want more—go to iancaskey.com.

ACKNOWLEDGMENTS

To Brent Robison and Tom Newton of Recital Publishing: many thanks for your publication of this work and your help bringing it to completion.

To those who inspired me with their own writing, read a story or two or more from this work, and provided insight: Adam Berlin, Timothy Brandoff, Shelley Stenhouse, Ben Pryor, Sean Madigan Hoen, Leslie Maslow, Mike Gardner, David McClelland, Adrian Scheer Rieder, Kate Lutzner, Erika Lutzner, Cynthia Weiner, Doris Vila Licht, Maria Baker, Laura Tucker, Andrew Lenza, Joliange Wright, John Greenburg.

To those who helped me believe: Nicole Reed, Amos Poe, Mark Evans, Matt Whyte, Rich Sandomeno, Bentley Wood, Matt Sweesy, Brian Kalkbrenner, Greg Ames, Jeff Jackson, Jason Burgin, Allen Zadoff, Robin Amos Kahn, Colin Beavan, Mary Davis, Joshua Jordan, Kohl Sudduth, James Beaudreau, Brad Truax, Jason Sebastian Russo. And the ever-divine Harriet Powers!

To these authors whose work inspired this work: Roberto Bolaño, Richard Ford, Arthur Bradford, Christine Schutt, Maryse Meijer, Brian Evenson, Paul Bowles, James Purdy, Jerzy Kosinski (Steps!), Roland

Topor, Welles Tower, Enrique Vila-Matas, Jess Walter, and Stewart O'Nan.

Special thanks to my great grandmother—a folklorist of the Hispanic Southwest and children's book author: Aurora Lucero White Lea.

MORE INFORMATION

Other Books from Recital Publishing

Our Lady of the Serpents by Petrie Harbouri

Voyages to Nowhere: Two Novellas by Tom Newton

The Lame Angel by Alexis Panselinos

The Joppenbergh Jump by Mark Morganstern

Ponckhockie Union by Brent Robison

Seven Cries of Delight & Other Stories by Tom Newton

Saraceno by Djelloul Marbrook

The Principle of Ultimate Indivisibility by Brent Robison

A Request

If you enjoyed this book, its publishers and author would be grateful if you would post a short (or long) review on the website where you bought the book and/or on Goodreads.com or other book review sites. Thanks for reading!

~ Please visit us at **RecitalPublishing.com**. ~

Made in the USA
Monee, IL
19 November 2021